# ARTEMIS

## RISING

EMMA HODGSON

# ARTEMIS

## RISING

TATE PUBLISHING
AND ENTERPRISES, LLC

Published by Tate Publishing & Enterprises, LLC
127 E. Trade Center Terrace | Mustang, Oklahoma 73064 USA
1.888.361.9473 | www.tatepublishing.com

Tate Publishing is committed to excellence in the publishing industry. The company reflects the philosophy established by the founders, based on Psalm 68:11,
*"The Lord gave the word and great was the company of those who published it."*

Book design copyright © 2013 by Tate Publishing, LLC. All rights reserved.
*Cover design by Jan Sunday Quilaquil*
*Interior design by Honeylette Pino*

Published in the United States of America

ISBN: 978-1-62854-204-2
1. Fiction / Fantasy / General
2. Fiction / Fairy Tales, Folk Tales, Legends & Mythology
13.08.23

Dedicated to my loving family
To my mom and sister for helping me keep the
motivation to finish this book.
Thank you to everyone who supported
me in fulfilling my dream.

# Chapter One

I stood under the balmy Texas heat. The sun on Mike's front lawn sent blinding rays of sunshine into my eyes. I sighed. I know they thought this was a good idea in the beginning, but what did they know? I walked over toward the others in terror.

"Oekapa!" I cursed in ancient Greek. I could see this would not end well, but Zeus was not going to let me win this battle. Not if he could help it.

The day this ludicrous plan had been set into motion was during the last summer solstice. I sat on Olympus digging my nails into my throne as the other gods all agreed to the order. I just sat there making sure that each one of them got a dirty look of disgust from me. Zeus had come up with one of his brilliant plans; all the major gods would separate all over the world disguised as high school students. Apparently, it would help us understand the human condition better. I thought human teenagers weren't meant to be understood. To me it was just another way for Zeus to prove to us how powerful he was. When they all caught on to my stares, Zeus fired, "Artemis, do you accept?"

"Well, humor me, what would you do if I said, no?" I spat back at him. He came up blank. No one ever challenged his plans. Not out loud anyway. "No?" His voice boomed with shock. "Sorry to disappoint you almighty one," I sneered sarcastically. Apollo, my twin brother, looked worried. I just gave him a you-better-keep-your-mouth–shut-or-you're-going-wake-up-with-an-arrow-through-your-head look. He responded with one of his famous toothy grins.

Zeus watched with frustration as I glanced around the circle of thrones that held the twelve major gods. On the largest gold throne sat Zeus, king of the gods, lord of the skies. He wore a clean, white suite embroidered with lightning bolts that seemed to gleam with electricity. To his right sat his wife Hera, queen of the gods, and goddess of marriage and women, which was ironic considering the growing list of her husbands mortal mistresses. To Zeus's left sat his older brother Poseidon, the god of the seas. Then there was Ares, god of war. Moving down the circle sat Apollo, my twin brother and god of archery, the sun, medicine, music and prophecy. Next, slouching in his chair sat Hephaestus. As a baby, his mother Hera threw him off Olympus because he was born imperfect with a shriveled foot. I have never actually seen the foot – I have only heard stories about it. He was only allowed to return when he showed amazing talent melting metal into shields and weapons. He became the god of fire and metalworking. Then there was Dionysius, as drunk as can be, holding a golden wine goblet in his trembling fingers. He was the god of wine and parties. He was almost never seen completely sober and dressed in loud, obnoxious clothes that stood out from the usual white everyone else wore on Olympus. Next to him sat a more subdued Hermes. Most know him as the messenger of the gods but most don't know that he got stuck with being the god of seemingly everything else, too. Seriously, he is also god of traveling, crossroads, inns, thieves, treaties, commerce, sports, and border crossings. He and Apollo always fought over who really was the god of more things, but the arguments usually led nowhere.

On the other half of the circle sat Aphrodite, goddess of beauty and love. Her beauty always overtook the room, and she knew it. Next to her was Athena, goddess of wisdom and strategy. Athena was like Ares' smarter half. While he would charge straight into battle without thinking, she would plan her attacks with logic and precision. Then there was me, Artemis. I am the goddess of the moon, archery, hunting, and maidens. Not a bad list for me. I love my goddess role and my ability to summon my huntresses as I please. Finally, sitting next to Hera was Demeter, the goddess of the harvest and seasons.

"Sorry Artemis but this is not an option. You are required." Zeus spoke quickly, trying to keep his temper in check. I rolled my eyes but nodded. I had expected no less. From across the room I could hear Aphrodite giggle. I whipped my head to scowl at her, which by this time I had mastered to an art form.

We were told to go put our names on the country or state of our choice. I stared at the sign-up sheets. Really? Gods needed sign-up sheets? Why did no one think this plan was demeaning except for me? Zeus was a manipulative leader. He always had some point he was trying to make but he rarely let anyone know what the point was. I was in the unenviable position of disagreeing with his plan. I just didn't really understand. Why did we need to understand the human condition better? Especially the teenage human condition. We were gods and goddesses, comfortably separated from humans. Zeus didn't do anything without a purpose, and that purpose usually was for his own benefit. I couldn't figure out what his reasoning was behind this plan. And, I wasn't sure he wanted me to understand. So, I decided to be disagreeable.

I tested Zeus again with a sneer; I hoped he would understand this as an attempt to rethink this plan. No luck. He stormed out, and I was left staring at my eventual fate—a sign up sheet. The others were busy following his orders. I wasn't sure what I should do. With my bad attitude intact, I decided to take a look. The sign-up sheets had identified specific schools across the globe for us to choose. A good, teenage education is what was intended for us. I didn't understand any of it but I decided to play along like the rest of my fellow rulers. You see, you didn't really want to disagree with Zeus. It rarely went well for those who did. Many mortals, back in the times when gods were worshiped, had seen the end of Zeus's bolts for defying his plans. I didn't want to end up like the charred souls that had dared to question what he demanded.

I glanced around the table and the descriptions looked as dreadful as I had imagined. Then, I suddenly was drawn to the sign-up sheet marked, *United States, Texas*. It was definitely big enough, sunny, and supplied very good hunting. I guess I could make it fun. I think I had some distant relations there, somewhere. I wasn't sure. Gods and humans had previously interacted, and I knew Texas was part of my family heritage. Plus, it was far enough away from Washington D.C. In the capital city lays the U.S entry to Olympus. Most people have never seen it but on the top of the White House is a hidden stairwell that leads you straight to the top of Olympus. Every country in the world has an access portal to Olympus. Some are in random street alleys, and others are in palaces where you can transcend space and time to place you at Olympus. In England, the portal resides inside Big Ben. In Egypt, the portal is part of the Sphinx, and in Paris, it is underneath the Eiffel tower. All demigods were taught the exact locations throughout the world so they could have quick access the real Mt. Olympus, which is the highest mountain in Greece and the home to the Greek gods.

This meant that every President since the United States government was built has known about the world of the gods and their demigod children. A demigod is a child born of a human and a god. Supposedly the U.S. Presidents come into the White House without any knowledge we exist, and they leave the White

House knowing more than they imagined. I believe they have debriefings about the existence of gods and our monsters on the same evening. No wonder U.S. Presidents age faster than other humans!

So I decided Texas was going to be the place for me. I mean, if I had to go. I still made sure I let everyone around me know I thought the whole idea was insane. One of the perks of being a god is that you get to avoid the teenage years, and now I was going to be forced to experience them for an entire year! I decided if I had to do this, I was going to do it on my own terms, so I created my entire identity to present to Zeus for his approval.

I would go to San Antonio, Texas, as a seventeen-year-old girl named Bryn Davidson. As a Greek god, I, like the other gods, can shift into any form I wish, at any time. For this assignment, I have chosen platinum blonde wavy hair, fair skin, shimmering amber eyes, and a healthy height of 5 feet 8 inches tall. I'm not going to choose to go into this as a gawky fourteen year-old. If I must do this, I am going to go in looking good and hopefully out of the awkward phase. I would be a senior at South West Academy.

Zeus approved my plan and chuckled at my choice. I wasn't sure why, but I pretended not to notice. Our assignment was to live our lives for one year as teenage students in high school. I was supposed to learn how humans act and to perfect my "human side." We had plenty of exercises on Mount Olympus to improve our "god side," but we had never attempted to become great humans. We could shoot arrows for untold miles. We could mount horses and fly through the air. Some of us could swim underwater for hours. But, none of us had learned how to harness the art of human emotion. When Zeus had approved my plan, he handed me a packet of papers lined in gold. The papers stated that I would be living in the Watermark Hotel in downtown San Antonio. I was to tell people, if asked, that I lived there with my mother. The papers described my room as Suite 394. In the room I would find a credit card, US Currency, a high school transcript, a cell phone, clothes, and the keys to a car, which would be registered in the valet of the hotel. I felt odd about the thought of living in a small, cramped room. It was a trapping feeling to know that everything would already be laid out and chosen for me. I had a strong feeling I was going to be spending very little time at the Watermark.

# Chapter Two

I shuffled my way down the dimly lit hallway to my first period class; the first class on my schedule was English Literature in room 203. I sharply inhaled and gripped the metal door handle and thrust it open. The scene inside was horrifying. Kids were sitting on their desks, some dashing around and knocking over chairs, while a group of sneering girls were laughing and pointing at other girls across the room. They seemed to be talking about something that had happened the weekend before to one of the girls in the other group. I ducked my head, desperately trying not to draw any attention to myself and took a seat next to a redheaded girl in black skinny jeans and a cheesy shirt that read, "Theater is my Life!" She seemed like someone I could bear to be around. "Hi, my name is, Art—, Bryn." I stumbled over my new name. The girl smiled. "Hey, Bryn! I'm Brooke. Are you new here?" she asked smiling. No. I'm just now coming out of the box in the corner that I have been in all year.

"Yes, I came here from...Washington, D.C." I wasn't exactly lying, but Mt. Olympus was probably a more accurate answer. "Awesome. So Bryn, what are you into?" she looked me over as if the answer might be hidden somewhere on my face. Oh you know, being the goddess of the moon and hunting. I also enjoy fighting monsters with my band of immortal huntresses. I decided to keep that to myself.

"*Uhm.*" I at least wanted to try and fit in. "Theater," I finally said. "Really? Me too! You should totally consider trying out for the Spring play!" she said with too much enthusiasm. "Um, yeah, sure. Sounds great." One step at a time Artemis. Try to at least make this enjoyable. "Great," I managed. "See you there!" she exclaimed.

After English class ended, I made it through math and science with ease. I was surprised how much I knew or remembered. I can't remember ever being formally taught math and science, but I knew everything that was being taught as if I had been in a class before. My next class was Latin. I already knew the language, so I thought it would be an easy A.

As I walked into my Latin class, I stopped dead in my tracks. He stood in the classroom, staring at the white board, leaning back onto the desk behind him. My breath caught in my lungs, and I felt a strange breathless sensation. I searched over his face. He was attractive, sure, but a lot of men were attractive. He seemed to stick out to me for some reason, and I felt inexplicably drawn to him. My mind was racing. I have seen millions of men in my years. I had pushed them aside, sworn I could never love them; they would only hold me back from my goddess responsibilities. Part of my covenant as a goddess with my huntresses was to never become involved with a man. It got in the way of our hunting as I could never focus on my duties if I was distracted by a man. I had certainly been tempted in the past, but I always managed to avoid romance in my life. I was not going to let anything happen, but this was definitely going to be difficult.

I ran quickly to the farthest chair from him and turned to talk to a girl I recognized from my math class named Claire. She had a high-pitched voice and enthusiastic demeanor. As she spoke to me, I pretended to listen while I secretly watched as his eyes found their way over to me. He was making my I'm-a-goddess-so-I-can-just-pretend-you-don't-exist frame of mind extremely difficult. I interrupted Claire and whispered, "Who is he?" I pointed toward *the* boy. He had long brown hair that just skimmed his eyebrows and a perfect godly smile. Trust me, I would know. He had the most brilliant baby blue eyes. He was absolutely drop-dead gorgeous. He was the kind of guy who you thought it wasn't fair he was a guy because he was just so—beautiful! Claire's lips tugged at the edges. "Cute, right? His name is Landon Matthews. Don't get your hopes up, though. You're not his type. No one seems to really be his type. Trust me, many have tried." I wasn't planning on getting my hopes up for him, nor had I ever considered being anyone's type. But he was likely the most attractive boy I had ever seen, and I couldn't make my eyes stay away from his. Maybe being a human teenager might be fun after all.

When the bell rang I knew I couldn't waste a second gathering my things. Face-to-face time with Landon was definitely not what I needed right now. My goal was to survive this one-year of high school, and then I would be done. I'm a goddess. I can fight monsters with my bare hands and have endured thousands of years with Zeus. I can handle blue eyes and beautiful white teeth. Right? Just as I was about to answer my own question, he walked over to introduce himself.

"Hi. I'm Landon Matthews." He stuck his hand out as he spoke. His voice was smooth and sweet as a lullaby. "You are so beautiful, I just had to come over and say hello." He grinned and looked straight through me. Oh great, he's a flirt. "Thanks Landon, I'm Artemis." My heart stopped beating for a fraction of a second. If you don't start getting your new name right these people are going to start getting suspicious.

"Artemis..." He paused. "Like the goddess?" "Not exactly, but it's kind of embarrassing," I said. Not that I have actually ever felt embarrassment, but I was on a roll. "That's what my friends in D.C call me because I'm really into mythology, and she was always my favorite. My real name is Bryn." I was rambling on now but my lie seemed to make sense. He touched his finger to my lips to silence me. "It's OK Bryn." He brushed my hand with his. I couldn't decide if his touch was intentional or not. I hoped it was an accident. Kind of. My palms started to sweat. That had only happened once in my life when I was actually running for my life during a hunt that had gone terribly wrong. What was happening to me? Was I already starting to feel like a teenager? I had barely gotten through four classes on my first day!

"And, she was always my favorite, too." I'm not sure how long he had been talking, but I realized he was talking to me and about me. Great, he was one of my biggest fans. I smiled, and when I said I had to go to lunch, he offered for me to eat at his table with him. By the look in his crystal eyes, I could tell he was not going to take no for an answer. I agreed and timidly walked beside him on my way toward the lunchroom. He was not making this easy.

The lunchroom had about twenty separate, dark oak tables. Landon led me to the one in the dead center. At one of the tables, I watched a couple of guys hunch over their cell phones. At another table sat girls wearing shorts that were way too short – even for teenagers. They admired themselves in their mirrors. I literally almost gagged. Apparently, I didn't keep my emotions to myself as Landon cracked a smile and laughed. "They aren't so bad. You might actually like them!" The Aphrodite-type teens had not even uttered a syllable, and I already loathed them. Suddenly I missed my hunters. They were real. And tough. And they focused on things that mattered. I sighed aloud. I don't think I was doing it on purpose, but I seemed to be making sure everyone around me knew I was miserable.

"Guys, this is Bryn!" Landon smiled his signature smile. It jolted me out of my funk, and I suddenly wanted to be exactly where I was. I almost melted. I kept myself together by focusing on Brooke, one of the girls I had met in my English lit class. She was sweet, pretty, and an interesting person I could spend time with. There was something about her I liked, but I couldn't figure out what it was. Brooke made me feel comfortable, and I needed some comfort at this point in my day!

As I readjusted back into my human reality, I was visually assaulted by a bleach-blonde girl who stood uncomfortably close to Landon and kept glancing between us. "Well Bryn, it seems you have really cast a spell on Landon here." Her words dripped with disdain. "This is very impressive considering your mom jeans, baggy shirt, and biker boots," she mocked.

Landon cringed. "Well Alicia, aren't you the charmer?" Landon spat back, and then turned to me, "I'm sorry Bryn; she has issues." He winked.

"Well, isn't that the sweetest thing ever. Right, Katy?" Alicia turned toward the brunette who was reapplying her mascara using her iPhone screen as a mirror. "*Um*, sure." Katy stumbled over her words, apparently trying to keep her leader happy. My whole world froze in that moment. I had never been addressed in this way before, and I could feel my blood boiling under my skin. I stood up straighter and looked the girl directly in the eyes. "I'm not sure who you think you are," I spoke slowly, letting every ounce of power I had drip into the words I was saying. "But I would be extremely careful if I were you. I am not someone you want as an enemy." I pulled my eyes away from the girl, and begun to turn away. I walked away slowly from the table, making sure to keep a strong presence about me, I wasn't going to be trampled over by some mortal girl with jealousy issues. I could hear Landon following me, but I swore to myself I would not fall for Landon or any other wide-eyed boy on this campus. No matter how cute he was.

# Chapter Three

The rest of the week went by slowly, but I managed. Ignoring Landon was difficult, but living with a bunch of Greek gods who had competing egos larger than life had taught me patience. I found myself hanging out with Brooke almost everyday. We laughed a lot, and I realized why I felt so natural when I was with her. She reminded me a lot of my twin brother Apollo.

I spent most of my free time hunting monsters. I would drive my new car outside the city limits with my bow by my side. I searched for any monster available, dragons or whatever happened to appear. It calmed my mind and reminded me of home. There were plenty of demigods around, which meant there were dozens of monsters, too. Hunting was the one thing that gave me joy. Immediately after school, I would bolt out of the building to enjoy the rest of the night hunting in the South Texas Hill Country. Dragons seemed the most abundant of the creatures. The scorching Texas weather attracted them, while cold dwelling monsters never set foot into the 106-degree weather. The rolling landscape was serene and beautiful. I was a teenage-high-school student by day, a goddess of the hunt by night. I knew this wasn't what Zeus had intended, but my instincts were too strong. I thought I already knew everything I needed to know about the human teenage condition from my first week in high school. I would stay in school and do as I was instructed, but there was nothing to hold my attention inside of those school walls. I was determined to get through, but learning wasn't on my mind. I honed my skills as a huntress because, however human I am right now, I was still a goddess.

The only bright spot during my teenage day was my time with Brooke. I felt like I was truly her friend, and I enjoyed the times we hung out. On Wednesday of week two, she asked if I would like to go shopping with her. I reluctantly agreed. I was happy to spend time with Brooke, but I couldn't imagine wasting an afternoon shopping. I knew Zeus would see my shopping spree as an act of submission to his mission, so I relented. I was confident an afternoon with Brooke would be fun, no matter where we spent it.

As a goddess, I was rarely swept up in human situations. I grew up around people just like me, so I never had to worry about things like human temptations and impulses— or bad teenaged decisions. Taking a goddess and a mortal to a public place, like a mall with lots of people, was the first time I knew that Zeus's plan was beginning to work. I started to act like a teenager, impulsively. We gods attract monsters, big ones that were designed to kill. When I hunted monsters alone in the Hill Country, my senses were focused on the hunt so it was fun. Sporty. If I had to fight a monster in the middle of a crowded mall, I feared it would not end well. But being the dutiful teenager, I ignored my better instincts and went anyway.

We walked around a strip mall, and I actually started to have fun trying on Brooke's choices of funky clothes. I swear this girl had more fashion sense in one finger than I did in my whole body. She had me trying on dresses and mini skirts. I tried to smile through the pain of actually looking like a real girl. Even though a lot of the clothes made me cringe, I was having a great time. Brooke and my brother were so similar. They both had wickedly funny senses of humor and could make me constantly giggle. I loved the feeling of being lost in the silly moment with Brooke as I had often done with Apollo. I was busy thinking about something Brooke said and suddenly, it was there, a stupid hellhound. It was a giant, vicious dog from the depths of the Underworld. I had my bow and arrows in my purse, but whipping that out in the middle of a packed mall was not a wise move.

I knew the mortals could not see the giant dog with bloodthirsty red eyes. Human brains had been wired to skip over things they could not explain. There are stories that at one point in history humans could actually see the demons we see. We were told about how humans began to call each other crazy and kill anyone who admitted to seeing the ferocious beasts. Call it evolution or whatever you want, but over time humans just stopped seeing them altogether. They would see something; they just didn't see it in its true form. They saw something that they could explain. So, instead of seeing an evil hellhound, they saw a dangerous-looking stray dog.

I have encountered some rare mortals who are able to see the beasts we see. I was hoping nobody around would be one of those poor souls today. I prayed that some violent demigod would run in and kill it. I couldn't rely on that to happen as the giant canine stood glaring at me. I turned to face the overpriced racks of clothes. I picked up a pink sparkly tank top and thrust it towards Brooke, hoping she wouldn't spot the hellhound outside the shop.

As the shirt hit Brooke, I heard her gasp. I cringed. "Sorry," I said, acting like it was an accident. "Not the shirt, that!" she pointed to the hound that was advancing toward us. "What in the name of all things holy is that? It's like five feet tall!" Great, she, of all people, had the clarity only a handful of humans have. Or, is she a demigod? No, by now I would have known, and she would definitely recognize a hellhound when she saw one. Hades, the god of death and the Underworld loves to turn hellhounds on demigods for sport. He held the same grudge against the demigods as he did their godly parents. After being given the full-time position of babysitting the dead, he had been trapped in the Underworld. He resented us for being able to live freely on Olympus, and he took it out on the other god's children. If she were a demigod she would not have been shocked by the appearance of this beast. I grabbed for my bag, but unfortunately I was too slow. The hellhound burst its way through the door, sending glass shards everywhere. Brooke let out a blood-curdling scream.

It was ripping through the clothes to get to me. It leaped through the racks of shirts and dresses with its giant claws thrashing through air. Its eyes were red as blood and it sent mannequins flying and smashing to the ground. I struggled with my bow as it tried to come out of my enchanted purse. The dog moved closer, and I finally freed my arrows. I launched a volley of silver arrows into the creature's heart, and it fell dead to the floor, leaving the mess behind. Hellhounds don't actually die. They were made of shadows—atoms of darkness held so closely together they could wreak untold havoc. When they were 'killed' they simply dissolved back into the dark shadows that created them. "Holy—" I didn't let Brooke finish that statement; I hit her on the head with the butt of my bow, knocking her out cold. I took her to a different store and pretended she tripped and hit her head on a shelf. She's known to be a world-class klutz, so I thought my story would pass.

I sat with her and held the back of her head as if she had fallen on her own. I waited a few moments until she awoke. She mumbled something about a giant killing dog and then her eyes snapped open. "What the French toast just happened?" Her eyes darted back and forth. I laughed at her choice of words and breathed a sigh of relief. I hoped I hadn't hit her too hard, and was thankful when her eyes opened. "You tripped and hit your head on the shelf." I pointed to the large white shelf in the corner. I could see deep in her eyes that she didn't buy it, but instead she laughed. "Sounds like me; I had the strangest dream though!" Her face was lost in thought.

"Here," I offered a hand and helped her up, "that's a pretty big bump. We should get you home." I smiled and patted the growing lump rising on her head. "Maybe next time we should try something a little less dangerous." She giggled, "Yah, I never thought I would need to wear a helmet to go shopping!" I laughed along and drove her home. "I had a great time, Brooke!" I said as I left to go back to my new home. "We should do this again sometime! See you at school!" She said something, but I had already rolled up the window so the south Texas heat wouldn't kill me.

As I drove, I thought about my assignment and still wondered what Zeus was trying to teach us. Zeus always had a plan. Most of his plans were designed to fuel his own ego, but I couldn't figure this assignment out. Was I really just trying to experience the human condition from the vantage point of a human teenager? It still didn't make sense to me. But, true to my teenage form, I actually felt so hungry it distracted my thoughts. Gods don't technically need to eat, but we still enjoy it. Ambrosia and nectar—that kind of thing. But today I had my eye on a TexMex restaurant, Paloma Blanca, which all my friends raved about. As soon as I pulled into the restaurant, there he was. Landon. The perfect specimen of a teenage boy. I was hungry, but not for drama. This was not what I needed.

"Bryn!" He called running over to meet me. After a quick hug, he faced the lady at the counter. "She will be joining our table." Then he grabbed my wrist and pulled me toward the group. At the small table sat the same bunch of kids from lunch the first day. Oh joy! "Hi," I spoke weakly.

"Hey, Bryn!" The guys called in unison from the table.

I got a very dirty look from Alicia, and then she spoke.

"Oh, hi. Please excuse me, I have to take this." She pointed to her silent phone. "Have fun speaking with your imaginary friends, Alicia!" Landon laughed as he watched her scramble up from the table. She stormed out of the restaurant. Once she disappeared, the whole table burst into a fit of laughter. I found it odd how Landon tried to stand up for me in his strange, mocking way. I was so used to people being afraid of me, and their fear had always kept them a comfortable distance away. My reputation had caused them to always keep up a veil of terrified politeness. I had always seemed to enjoy the space it put between me and the rest of the world. Until now.

"Well," Landon spoke between laughs, "You never actually got to meet everyone and since the 'Wicked Witch of the West' just left, allow me to introduce you." He smiled, "This is Patrick, Evan, and Mike." Patrick had long blonde hair that reached his chin and dimples a mile wide. Evan had short black hair and his brown eyes looked like they were gazing into your soul. Mike was altogether different with short, crazy brown hair and a huge crooked smile. He looked exactly like my brother. I stood there in shock, as if I had seen a ghost. Was I just missing my old life or was everyone reminding me of Apollo? Twins sometimes have unusual sensations where they think alike, and I was wondering if this was just a twin thing. I looked more closely at Mike, and I was sure this was not a twin coincidence. This kid looked so much like Apollo it was shocking.

I looked down to his neck where a small sun-shaped necklace hung, the sign of my brother. The sign of Apollo, god of the sun, was hanging around this boy's neck. I knew Apollo had a demigod son. Apollo spoke of him, but I had never actually met him. Maybe Apollo's discussions and descriptions of South Texas were what had attracted me here in the first place. Maybe seeing him was part of Zeus's plan? I had no idea, I just knew this boy who was sitting across the table from me was my twin brother's son. A demigod— part god, part human. I had to find out if I was crazy or if this boy was really who I thought he was. Who I *knew* he was.

Landon was busy still introducing everyone, but I was completely fixated on Mike, his necklace, and the fact that he had my brother's face.

"Then the girls," Landon kept talking, "Katy, Louisa, and Morgan." They all smiled.

"Sorry about being rude," Morgan whispered as if Alicia might hear, "Alicia can be such a jerk." The night went on happily. Alicia never returned and nobody seemed to miss her. We exchanged numbers, laughs, and embarrassing moments. Under the table, I texted

Mike. I had only seen that necklace once in my life and I was sure there weren't any duplicates.

Bryn: Son of Apollo?
Mike: Hwd u know?
Bryn: Necklace
Mike: Oh...u?
Bryn: I'm not a demigod
Mike: Then what?
Bryn: I'm Artemis
Mike: WHAT!?!
Bryn: Yeah
Mike: Well...that's awkward.
Bryn: Why?
Mike: I kinda thought u were cute...
Bryn: I think that's illegal
Mike: Moving on, y r u here...Aunt?
Bryn: You know, Zeus's plan
Mike: Yuck :P Srry. We'll tlk later.

I smiled. It felt good for someone to know, even if it was just my brother's son. I tried to ignore what I felt for Landon and the fact that I was suddenly sitting across the table from my nephew I had never met. I would find time to talk to Apollo and Mike later. Tonight, I focused on making friends so I could fit in and enjoy my year in high school. I knew it was what I was there to do, and for the first time, it actually felt right.

The conversation was slow-paced and comfortable, and I was able to join in occasionally with out spilling anything of importance. "So, Bryn, how are you enjoying Texas so far?" Evan asked, quickly swallowing his food.

"Fine. The heat is a little brutal." I smiled over at him.

"You never really get used to it. Honestly, I have lived here my entire life and the heat still shocks me." Patrick smiled sadly before swiping his long hair out of his eyes. "Landon here says you are from Washington D.C. What's it like up on Capitol Hill?"

"A lot more commotion, I assure you." I quickly skimmed over the details. I had never technically lived there, and I was a little rough on the daily lives of those who did. Evan smiled over at Patrick, and they began a ten minute story about their trip up there last summer.

When the conversation lulled again I looked over at Landon, "So you told them where I came from? What else have you told them?" Everyone laughed.

"Your entire life story! Everything you have ever done or thought about doing. The entire school knows by now," Landon joked, and I smiled warmly at him. I was suddenly fearful that if he really knew me well he wouldn't be so keen on keeping up this conversation. What was wrong with me?

"We know every past boyfriend you have ever had. Landon plans on destroying them all." Morgan smiled lightly and then winked over at Landon. I could see the pink of his blush creeping up his neck. I laughed with her, even though if that were true Landon would have no one to kill.

"Not a fan of friendly competition, are you?" I joked.

"Not when it comes to you." Landon smiled and I heard the three boys groan.

"Landon, that's just lame, my friend." Evan rolled his eyes before turning back to his food.

"It was sweet! Cut him a break!" Louisa smiled at me, her long black hair falling into her face. "It's not like you three have any game." Katy snickered, but was silenced by the glares from the boys.

"I have plenty of game, even though I would never use the word game," Evan spat.

"What with your pillow?" Patrick laughed giving, Mike a knowing nudge.

"And how would you know, Patrick?" winked Katy. I watched the quick banter flutter around the table until I felt dizzyingly out of the loop. I wasn't sure what "game" meant in this context, but it seemed like something Apollo would say. Soon we were all stuffed, and we walked out the door into the cool night. The conversation continued on the curb for a good ten minutes.

"I'm glad you happened by." Landon smiled down at me. "I want you to teach me that skill you have of getting Alicia to leave."

"I just have that way about me." It felt weird having this sort of conversation with a guy. Not uncomfortable, just new. "I don't know what it is about you, Landon. You're not like the others." The words spilled out of my mouth before I could stop them.

"Well neither are you." *You could say that*, I added mentally. "I hope I can get to know you better. Bryn, do you want me to drive you home?" Landon asked with a hopeful grin.

"Actually, Landon," Mike appeared behind us, "Bryn's mom knows mine and she's at my house right now. Bryn has her own car, and she has offered to take me home." Wow, I thought. He can tell a sweet lie just like his dad. A chip off the old block! "Oh." Landon's face fell, "OK! Well, see you tomorrow, Bryn!" He smiled and grabbed my hand. I knew to feel this way was wrong, but dear gods! Chills ran through me. His smile told me he felt it, too. Was this part of Zeus's plan? I was pretty sure the answer to that was no.

"Bryn," Mike's voice brought me back, "let's go." I stumbled into the car. "Dear Zeus! You're exactly like your dad," I told him. He looked wryly at me and admitted, "That's what my mom always say about me! So wait, you don't look like Artemis. Why is that?" I closed my eyes and shifted back into my real form of long black hair, coffee-colored eyes, and a glow of power. I wore the shimmering silver robes that I had worn at Olympus.

"There. Is that better?" I asked. My voice had dropped an octave. "Wow," Mike gasped, "I would bow if I weren't sitting in a car!" "That's not necessary. So where are we going?" I whispered. He nodded ahead, "To my house. You can meet my mom. She will be so excited to meet you. She is one of those mortals who can see things as they are. Where are you staying?" he asked. "The Watermark Hotel on the River Walk." I grimaced. It was a nice hotel but the Riverwalk in San Antonio was packed. Colorful shops and restaurants lined the small walkways that sat on either side of the river. Barges took people up and down the river constantly, and the bars stayed open all hours. There were way too many people for my taste.

"Well, now you are staying in our guest room. We have tons to talk about," Mike said with pride. "Great,"

I told him. "My brother will never leave me, will he? Even when he's thousands of miles away, his son seems to find me!" "No, ma'am!" Mike said with a cute Texas twang and turned up the radio and started to belt out the lyrics to "Hello, Goodbye" by the Beatles. You could feel the sunshine lighting through every one of his pores; I couldn't help but smile. It was very odd being commanded like that. I had never been told where to be, save Zeus on a rare occasion.

We pulled up to the driveway and Mike dashed out of the car to the door in record time. His house was a small two-story brick house; ivy grew up the sides giving it a sort of majestic feel. I sprinted to meet him. He thrust the door open, "Mom! Where are you?" "In here, Mike," she called and walked out from the kitchen. I could see why my brother had fallen for her; she was very tall, with long chestnut-brown waves that fell to her lower back. She had high cheek bones and warm, brown eyes.

"Is anyone else here?" he whispered. "No, why? And, who's at the door?" she whispered back, with concern tainted in her words. "Good! Mom, this is Artemis." I walked in. "Artemis? Like the Greek goddess? Oh, my," she stammered as I walked in.

"Yes, it's me. Hi, Mrs., Oh I never learned your last name." "Holly Gomez. You can call me, Holly."

"Great. Holly, I should probably explain why I am here." She nodded and sunk onto the sofa. Mike jumped in, and I sat across from them. "You see, Zeus has ordered us to disguise ourselves as human teenagers," I morphed into Bryn as I spoke, "and live through a year of high school to get to know human behavior better. I noticed your son's necklace, his father is Apollo, correct?"

"Wow, yes. Um, I don't really know what to say. You are beautiful. And Apollo. I haven't thought about him, in, well, I actually think about him every day. Mike looks exactly like him. Don't you think?" I don't think she really wanted an answer. She just kept talking. "I knew about you. Apollo talked about you. Did you know about Mike? Did Apollo tell you about us?" Before I could answer, she started talking again. "I'm sorry. You don't have to answer that. I just... it's just so good to see you. To meet you. You know you are welcome here as long as you would like." She sighed in relief as she finally stopping talking.

She put her arms around me in a hug that lasted too long for my comfort, but I know she meant well. She showed me to the guest room and made me promise I would stay with her. She clung to my hand, as if she had known me before, or was hoping to know me better. She could tell Mike and I were eager to talk. She gave her son a loving stare, filled with a ton of meaning that I could only try to decipher. I'm sure she wanted to make sure Mike treated me with respect, which I knew he would. And so did she. She grabbed my hand again and left the two of us to talk.

"So Bryn," Mike began, "Wait! Should I call you Artemis or Auntie?"

I laughed. "No, you can call me Bryn. I think it might be weird if you called me 'Auntie' at school."

"That's true, so first things first, Landon," he said. I cringed. "He's like in love with you and y'all have barely spoken to each other!"

"Speak of the devil." I mumbled as my phone lit up and Landon's number flashed on my screen. The phone had been in my hotel room for me when I first arrived, and I was still trying to figure it out. Brooke told me I could download things called apps but none of it made any sense. I was lucky I had learned how to send a text.

"Hah!" Mike laughed. "But you swore never to love a man, right? Isn't that the oath of Artemis? Not to be nosey, but I can tell you feel something. What are going to do?"

"That's the problem! I have no idea! For the first time in my very long life, I can't stop thinking about this boy. I feel like I'm going crazy. Oh, and by the way, I think Brooke can see through the veil." I assumed that being the son of Apollo, Mike would know the veil was the phenomenon where humans had created a block in their minds to allow them not to see what they couldn't explain.

I told him the story of our shopping trip gone wrong. Mike listened, and then he started peppering me with questions about why I was here. He knew a lot. He understood Zeus's enormous ego from stories Apollo had told him. He wanted to understand why we were sent here to live as temporary teenagers. He was asking questions faster than I could answer. Just then lightning struck the ground outside of the house.

"Watch your words," I whispered, "or next time that is going to be your head." I knew being in the company of Apollo's son, talking openly about Zeus's plan was going to attract his attention. We were under a tight gag order to keep our assignment a private affair among the gods. I kind of figured this was a loophole since I was talking to my brother's son. Guess not. Zeus made his point. But I still had to figure out how to manage Mike's knowledge and my new friend Brooke who could see things most mortals couldn't. My cover wasn't going to be easy to keep. And, I didn't enjoy lightning strikes dancing around my head in warning!

"I'm worried," I explained to my nephew. "I have no idea what to do about Brooke. She is going to get suspicious, if she is hasn't already caught on to something. Mortals like her live their whole lives seeing things they can't explain, probably thinking they are crazy. With me around, her crazy sightings are only going to get worse. It's only a matter of time before something worse than a hellhound attacks and does some real damage. I can only knock her out so many times."

"I have a plan!" Mike smiled with an evil grin.

"I probably don't want to hear it, but go on." My words were cut off by an overwhelming presence outside Mike's door. The power was so strong; we were frozen with fear. Zeus wasn't the only one who didn't like the idea of a god and a demigod conspiring together. I reached for my bow and Mike grabbed his sword off the mantel. We braced ourselves for what was coming.

# Chapter Four

I had never actually been this close to her. Echidna, the mother of all monsters. Echidna was an enormous creature who is part woman, part snake. Her face was beautiful, in a haunting sort of way. She wasn't beautiful like Aphrodite, but she had flowing hair that cascaded down to her slithering snake-like body. Her image was breathtaking. She was called the mother of all monsters because she supposedly had mothered every Greek monster we ever knew. Not exactly someone you want to run into on an afternoon stroll. My huntresses and I had fought her before, but she just kept finding me. "Bryn," Mike whispered, "What in the gods' name is that?"

"Um, a Greek monster called Echidna. We have a sketchy history. Just shoot her!" I demanded.

"With a sword?" he screamed. "You know what I meant; *stab her!*" I yelled as I switched into Artemis.

The beast roared as she swung her hand through the wall ripping out a huge chunk of drywall. The gaping hole exposed the sunlight and front yard into Mike's bedroom.

"I'm dead!" Mike declared as he stared at the hole ripped through his house. "Even if I live through this, I'm dead! I will have something worse than a Greek monster coming at me. I will have my mom!" Echidna roared and stepped through the giant hole in the wall. She kicked over the table sending it fifty yards into the stairs, missing me by a half an inch.

"Artemis-s-s" she whispered in her snake-like voice. "Did-d-d you not hear-r? Now that Zeus-s-s-s has separated the gods Hades-s-s has s-sent us-s to des-story all of you. He s-s-still is not over being *banisshhhed* to the Underworld. He will des-s-troy you and all you hold dear, and you will be the one to rot in Tartarus-s-s! All the gods-s-s will be killed at his-s-s hand-s-s, we will live free and Hades-s-s will rule."

"That plan will never work and you will die trying! Haven't we been over this before? You can't win. You aren't sending me to Tartarus because you would have to kill me first, and that is not going to happen. So I really do hope you enjoy your time rotting in the Underworld." I tried to sound confident, but my voice shook.

"Oh, Artmis-s-s-s I'm not worried. I will jus-st reform like all the other time-s-s you tried to kill me. And, you will rot in Tartarus with all of the other fallen gods. I can hardly wait!" Her body shook with laughter.

"We will see." I mumbled as I started to fire arrows into the monster's scales. Mike took my lead and charged the beast. He stabbed the monster's leg, but his sword just got caught in the scales, only agitating her. She roared and slashed through the air with her giant claws trying desperately to hit Mike. He tried to back away, but she crushed one of his feet under her tail and swiped her claws across his leg. Mike screamed in agony, and I gripped my bow harder. I shot five arrows into the monster's head. She was fast, much faster than I remembered, and she knocked most of the arrows to the ground. I reached for another, but before I could grab the arrow, she snatched my bow and crushed it underneath her feet. I rolled on the floor to avoid her giant claws. I grabbed Mike's sword and scrambled to avoid another swipe from her. I ran underneath her giant legs so she couldn't reach me. I jumped onto her leg and began to try to climb up her back. I couldn't fight her head-on, so I knew I had to attack from a different angle. I clawed my way up to her head. She screeched and grabbed around to try to remove me from her back. I took the sword and plunged it into her neck, but it just clinked against her tough scales.

Panicked, I looked for another opportunity. I could see an area where her armor receded. I thrust the sword under the scale and through her neck. She let out a final scream and fell to the ground. Her corpse fell into a large pile on the floor of Mike's bedroom. I hopped off of her body just in time. I quickly waved my hand over her, and she disappeared to the Underworld where she would rot, just as I had warned her she would.

"Ha! Send me to Tartarus? I don't think so," I rejoiced. I suddenly remembered Mike and quickly ran over to him. He was holding his leg and mumbling something under his breath.

"The enchilada got me! Taken down by Mexican food!" he yelled.

"Echidna," I corrected "and are you ok? We should get you to the hospital!"

"So we can explain that a giant snake-lady came and broke my house apart, and when we tried to defend ourselves, she ripped my leg open?" he laughed. I guess he was right. The cut was bad. It went from his hip all the way down to his knee, and it was stained by the dark violet hue of the poison, a large purple gash down to the bone. Not something we should exactly show a mortal.

"We can call your dad! He is the god of medicine for goodness sake. He can help us!" I told him excitedly.

"He is on some secret mission," Mike exclaimed. Then, I could see the realization take over his face. "Wait, he is on the same mission you are on! He told me he had some special work he was doing for Zeus. He is in some high school somewhere having the time of his life. How can he help us?"

"He's a god, Mike! He can be here in seconds, if he needs to be." I pulled out my phone and hit speed dial, number one.

"Hey sis," Apollo answered the phone after two rings, "How's Texas? Pretty cool we have cell phones, huh? I'm in Ohio, of all places. I didn't get to the sign-up sheets in time. I should have chosen California, or Hawaii," he continued. I interrupted him before he could go on."

"Apollo, will you shut up for five seconds! Your son is hurt!"

"What? Mike! I will be right there." His voice was suddenly very tense. In ten seconds flat, I could hear the roar of his car engine outside the door. The front door burst open, and he bounded up the stairs. His long, brown hair was wind-blown, and his usually very happy expression was replaced with one of worry. His brown eyes fluttered, and his mouth was set in a concerned scowl.

"Dad!" Mike called from his spot on the floor. He lifted his head off the floor to get a better look at his father.

"Mike." He looked relieved to see he was still able to move and speak.

"How did you get here so fast?" Mike looked excited, but Apollo ignored his son's question and walked over to see how badly he was hurt. He lifted Mike's leg off the floor and looked closely at the wound before gently placing it back down and whipping his head toward me.

"Artemis, how did this happen? This is an injury from Echidna. How did you get him involved with her?" he growled.

"I'm sorry, Apollo. She came after us. And, you should be proud of Mike. He seems to have the same battle strategy as you, charge headfirst and hope you don't die. Please tend to his wound, and I will tell you more. I can't watch that purple goo oozing out of his leg another second," I commanded as my voice quivered. I did not need the sun god to burst into flames. He leaned over Mike and whispered random words in Ancient Greek over him and pulled two small bottles from his pocket. He moved his hands over the wound and dropped fluid from the ancient bottles into Mike's open leg. In twenty minutes Mike was back on his feet and laughing with Apollo. As Mike gained his strength, they sat together and talked about life. Apollo was eagerly trying to catch up on what he had missed in Mike's life. I listened for a few minutes, and then I cleared my throat rather loudly to try and get them to stop talking.

"Apollo, we have a lot to talk about before you have to leave. I'm afraid Hades might be behind these attacks and is trying to take advantage of me while I am separated from the rest of the gods. The Echinda mentioned it before she attacked. He has sent the worst monsters he can find to try to kill me and put me in Tartarus." I tried to explain quickly, hoping Apollo would catch on. Hades is the god of the Underworld, death, and precious minerals like gold and silver. He wasn't really considered to be one of the twelve major gods in the Olympian court, but that was his own doing. He considered having to rule the Underworld as some sort of punishment. He would rather hide with the dead and only come up when necessary than have a good relationship with his brothers Zeus and Poseidon. As a result of his hate, he is cynical and constantly craving the revenge he thinks he so rightfully deserves.

"Well, when I saw my sister calling I was in the middle of a boring math lecture, information I already knew obviously. I saw you calling and took the opportunity to get out of math. I really did not expect any of this! My son is hurt, and Hades is plotting against you? I think I'm going to stop answering your calls!" He joked and Mike laughed. "So, how did you know Mike was my son, and why do you look like yourself?"

"I obviously did not want to fight the mother of all monsters as a seventeen year-old mortal girl. Oh, and his necklace. I recognized the gold sun necklace you gave to your son. That's enough chit chat bro. This is serious!"

"Settle down. Mike, I am so glad to know you are still wearing the necklace," Apollo beamed with pride at Mike as he spoke. His tone quickly changed as he looked at me and barked, "So, what's your plan?"

"What's *your* plan?" I spat back.

"I have no idea. I still don't understand why Zeus has us parading around as teenagers in the first place. Now Hades smells weakness and all hell is breaking loose. Literally. We are going to need to come up with a plan together. I can ditch the Ohio teenager thing and stay here with the two of you. We can do better together than apart," he suggested.

"No! Zeus would get to you sooner than Hades if you did that. Plus, I think your school would get suspicious if you suddenly disappeared." We all sat in silence for a minute thinking. Then Mike got a strange look on his face like he had just remembered something but wasn't sure if he should say it or not.

Suddenly he blurted, "Oh, and Artemis is falling in love. Well someone is in love with her, and I am pretty sure she likes him back!" My heart sank. I wasn't sure whether to pull out an arrow and shoot him or run and hide from Apollo. I knew his response would not be good. Apollo's face changed many times in the seconds he absorbed that information. First happy, then confused, to scared, and then something I could not read.

"Well done, sister. I don't know whether or not to throw a party or unleash the force of the sun on you. Though love is not going to kill you, I don't think, but Hades will. Let's not get too involved into our teenage character here and try to focus on staying alive and away from the Underworld. I don't have a plan yet, but I'm going to start by finding the other gods and telling them what we are up against. I'll call you later Mike. Tell your mom I said hi, ok? Thanks kiddo! I'll talk to you about this later Artemis, bye for now!" He flashed his legendary smile and ran towards his sports car sitting on the driveway and floored the gas. Just a few minutes later Mike's mom pulled up from her rundown truck. I could feel the edginess build in Mike as she got closer. He knew he was going to have to explain the destruction of his mother's home. As she stepped through the door, even I felt my heartbeat quicken. It was my fault her house was completely destroyed.

"Oh my God! What in the name of all things good and holy happened here Mike?" Holly yelled as she walked into her house. "Can I not leave you alone for two hours without something going wrong? What's that bandage around your leg? What happened? Why is the back door on the stairs?" She looked to the side of the house, which had been torn open. The couch was in shreds and purple goo was splattered all over the walls. The ivy that used to hang on the wall was now draped over the television, which also had a brick through the screen.

"Ummm...Dad says hi." Mike uttered.

"Your dad?" her voice seemed to become lighter as she spoke about Apollo.

"Holly," I started, "it was not Mike's fault. We believe Hades is trying to attack all the gods while we are separated and off Olympus. A Greek monster came and caused all of this. The monster came to hurt Mike and me. We fought and killed her, but Mike got hurt so I called Apollo to help heal him. That's all that happened." I mumbled trying to explain myself. Her face creased with worry.

"That's *all*?" She laughed, looking around. "I'm not sure what to say, Artemis. Can you fix this?" Holly pointed to the gaping hole in the wall. I nodded, feeling very embarrassed. With Mike injured and Apollo here, I had completely forgotten that the monster had left the house in shambles. I waved my hand over the hole, and it was immediately restored as if nothing had happened. All the pieces flew back to their rightful place, and all that was broken was restored. The whole house was back to the way it had been before. "I didn't think you could actually do that, but thank you. Michael, are you OK? You were hurt?" She cradled her son in her arms, and they walked together to another room. As they walked away, I noticed the front door had opened. Standing in the doorway was a small, redhead with her mouth open, her eyes bulging. I remembered I still had the form of Artemis, and my poor friend Brooke stood there staring at me. How was I going to explain everything to her?

# Chapter Five

"Brooke, how much of that did you hear or see?" I whispered. Brooke just stood there looking directly at me with an absolutely blank look on her face. I called out to Mike. My mind spun—she had no idea who I was! Would it be better to explain I was Bryn or just transform back into her? I quickly changed into Bryn and smiled wearily down at the confused redhead. I had hoped that would make her feel better. I was wrong. Her face lost all color, and I watched her sway slightly as if she was going to faint.

"Bryn?" she asked. Her words were barely audible. "Wh-what-what is happening? Who were you just a second ago? Why is Mike hurt? What—" She stumbled over the questions she could not explain and looked back and forth between Mike and me, desperately looking for an answer.

"I think it would be best if you sat down." Mike and I led her to the couch and sat her down. I handed her a pillow for her to clutch in case she got more freaked out. "Brooke, you know all the stories about gods and goddesses from ancient Greek mythology?"

"Like Zeus and Hera?" She mumbled. I cringed at the names. Not exactly my favorites.

"Yes. Brooke it's all real, every last myth. All true. It all happened, and the Greek gods and monsters are still alive today."

"Really?" She perked up as if someone had just given her a shot of caffeine. "That's awesome! That means I'm not crazy! For as long as I can remember, I have seen all these horrible monsters walking the streets. I knew no one else could see them, so I thought I was insane. One time I saw this random beast thing battle a monster. I just stood there in horror. No one else seemed to notice. Then, Bryn and I saw that huge dog, beast-monster-thing at the mall. I was supposed to think I fell, but I know I didn't. I have seen that beast before. Wait! Why can I see them, and no one else can?"

"Mortals can't see them" I explained, "Demigods, half-human, half-god, like Mike can see them. Though you are one of the few humans who can see through the veil most human brains create."

"Uh…what?" she asked.

"A long time ago when humans tried to forget about the gods and goddesses, anyone who still talked about the monsters they could see were killed. So people just pretended they couldn't see them and eventually their brains stopped recognizing them as monsters.

The humans would see them as something normal they could explain. Like a rabid dog, or a rogue bear. Some mortals are born with the ability to see through it, like you." Brooke let that sink in for a little while, still grasping the concept. Then suddenly her eyes lit up like she had just won the lottery.

"That is so cool! Wait, Bryn are you like me because you said Mike's the demigod, so that means you're not?"

"No, I'm not a demigod nor a human." As I spoke, her eyes went wide with fear.

"That means you're a monster? *Oh god*, Mike run! You hurt him. You are the one who hurt Mike!" Mike just stepped closer to me.

"Brooke, calm down!" Mike called, "She is not a monster. If Bryn was a monster, she would have killed us both already. She is a goddess, probably the farthest thing from a monster." Brooke's face lost its color again. She couldn't comprehend the information. I watched her glance toward the ground as if she was deciding whether or not to bow at my feet.

"It's official, I am going to need counseling," she mumbled to herself. She stared directly at me, deciding what to say. Then she exploded with questions, "Whoa! Who? What goddess? Are y'all serious? Do you look like this normally or that black-haired girl I saw at first? Why are you here? You should be on Olympus, right? Is that where you came from?" Her questions barreled out of her so quickly I could not understand a word she was saying. Mike and I burst into laughter.

"One question at a time Brooke!" I laughed, "Um, Artemis, yes we are serious, the black-haired girl. I'll explain why I'm here later, and yes I have lived my life on Olympus." Phew that was a lot to say in one breath.

"Artemis? Like goddess of moon and junk? So cool! So, you said Mike was a half-god, half-human? Is he, like, your kid?" she asked, wincing as she waited for my answer.

"No. Mike's father is my twin brother, Apollo," I explained as calmly as I could to try to bring her excitement level down a notch.

"Wait," she shouted. "If Apollo is Artemis' brother, uh, your brother that means Mike is your nephew?" she cringed as she asked.

"Yes! Now it's my turn to ask you something." I just had to know or it might kill me before Hades could." Why did you come here in the first place?" I had to know what she knew, so I could manage how mad Zeus was going to be and how much Hades knew.

"Well, you see I was still confused about our shopping trip and if that giant dog was real or not. I decided to ask you because it was eating at me. So I called your phone, but you didn't answer. I know you and Landon have sort of a thing," she continued. I flinched.

"No. We don't." She just rolled her eyes and continued on.

"So, I called him, and he said you were at Mike's house. He sounded really upset about that. Someone should probably tell him that Mike is your nephew. Anyway, I came over. Then I saw the hole in the wall and the black-haired girl fixing it." I sighed. She was putting everything together a little too quickly, and she wasn't going to stop with the questions. She was practically on fire with excitement. Her questions were coming at me in rapid succession.

"So, why aren't you married? Oh right," she answered herself, "you pledged to never love a man! Though, you have a thing for Landon, and he is in love with you." All the pieces were slowly fitting together in her head. "So even though you feel something, you can't be with him! Aw, it's like a tragic love story!" I laughed at the way she described the fix I was in. Tragic love story was not what I would have called it. A life-or-death battle with the Underworld was more like it, though I wasn't ready to feed Brooke with more information. She was obviously having a tough time with what she had already witnessed. I decided not to bring Zeus into it just yet.

"Tragic love story. Right." I smiled at my airheaded friend. Then I turned toward Mike. He had been strangely quiet this whole time, and it had started to worry me. I turned toward him to see his face struck with terror. "Mike, Mike what is it?" He didn't respond. He just stared at the front door.

"Hellhound." he whispered. I knew they were never going to leave us alone. The monsters kept finding me. I should just put a huge sign above my head that says: "I'm a goddess. Please monsters, come attack me!" But at this moment, it was not the hellhound that scared me. It was what was standing behind the hellhound that gave me chills.

A vampire-like demon stood leading the beast by a leash. I stood motionless and poised to fight. I was sure I hadn't seen this creature, an Empusa, in centuries. She was stunning to see. Her head and face were beautiful, in a devilish way. Her arms became wings, like that of a bat. The skin connecting her arms to her body was translucent, and you could see veins coursing through the skin. Her strong legs curved down to hooves where feet would normally be. She looked strong, mean, and fixated on Mike. Empusa are partial to feeding on men, counting on the Empusa's extreme good looks to seduce men to their deaths. An Empusa would cast a spell on a man and then feed on the blood of her victim. I was terrified for Mike as I saw the Empusa's stare fixated on him. I turned into Artemis and stood before the evil creatures. The hellhound lunged, trying desperately to sink his teeth into my skin.

"Now, Canis," the Empusa cooed at the hellhound, "Is that anyway to treat our host? You will have your turn, I promise. But not right now. Artemis it is just amazing to see you again darling! Wow it has been too long since we tried to kill each other last!" I suddenly recognized her as soon as she started to speak. I had fought her once before when she had come after my brother. If my memory served me right, which it always did, I won that battle. And I would win this one, too.

"Yes," I said in a mocking tone, "it has been too long since I have banished you to Tartarus. We will have to do this more often. I see your little dog Canis is doing well." As I spoke I pulled my bow back and shot a silver arrow through the head of the hellhound. "Oops, I guess it's time to go shopping for a new puppy." I said sweetly as her hellhound disappeared, leaving her holding an empty leash. Her face went red with anger.

"You should not have done that! Let me show you how battles are won dear Artemis," she said as she glared at me through her crimson eyes. She slowly turned toward Mike and put on the most seductive face she could manage through her rage. "Who are you handsome?" she cooed. Her voice was like liquid gold. Mike took a step closer to the evil demon.

"M-m-m-mike," he stuttered.

"Stay away from her Mike! She is a vampire demon. She is trying to trick you so she can suck your blood!" My words jolted him out of her spell, but I knew her seductive ways would overpower him. Mike looked confused, almost drunk with confusion and desire for her.

"Mike. What a strong, handsome name for a strong, handsome man!" she said to him as she opened her wings to try to envelope him in her grasp. "Come here, and give me a kiss. You know you want to. Just one little kiss. I won't hurt you." Mike slowly started to walk toward the demon. She stepped closer and ran her long fingers through his wavy hair. I turned toward Brooke to make sure she was still ok. Her face was filled with utter jealousy. Mike and Brooke? Yes, I could see that. She eyed the sword that was lying on the floor, and she lunged for it. Soon she was standing in front of the Empusa with the sword raised in front of her face.

"Hey she-devil! If you take another step toward Mike, the only thing you will be kissing is the end of my sword." Her eyes were on the edge of insanity. Mike's eyes snapped open. Brooke looked beautiful and brave as she faced the mighty beast. Mike's eyes lit up as Brooke stood in front of her. Brooke raised her sword above her head and thrust it downward into the demon's head, but she was not fast enough. The Empusa caught the blade before it slashed her in half. She was able to wrestle the sword away from Brooke, but she sliced her demon hand grabbing the blade.

"I don't usually feed on girls, but I can make an exception for you. I haven't killed a human in far too long. This will be a pleasure. It will warm me up for killing Artemis." She sang as she lunged for Brooke's neck. Brooke was small and nimble. She didn't stand a chance against the Empusa's strength, but as Brooke darted around the Empusa's legs, she lunged for Brooke and fell on her own sword. The lifeless body lay on the floor spewing gold blood. I waved my hand and the Empusa, along with the mess she caused, disappeared instantly.

Brooke dropped the sword to the floor and stared at the place where the Empusa had just been standing. "Wait. Where did she go?"

"She's dead?" Mike whispered as he scooped up Brooke into his arms. "You just saved my life!" he said as he leaned over and kissed her. Brooke giggled happily and leaned her head into Mike's chest.

"There is no way my nephew is dating my best mortal friend. That's just wrong!" I joked.

"Then look away." Mike laughed as he wrapped his arms around her waist and held her back to his chest. Brooke giggled again, and her cheeks flushed. Mike continued, "And it's worse for me because my best friend likes my aunt, who is a goddess, and he doesn't even know it. This is crazy!" We all looked at each other for what seemed an eternity, none of us was exactly sure how to react. Finally, Brooke's infectious giggle took over, and we were able to laugh for a moment. Brooke ended up in Mike's lap. They did look very happy. I watched how he looked at her, like she was the most amazing girl ever. I thought I had seen a glimpse of this look when they talked in math, but I could never have been sure, until now. It was beautiful to watch.

My thoughts suddenly drifted towards Landon. He was amazing, and he looked at me that way, too. I knew if I really wanted to I could repeal my law of never having a man in my life. To me, it would feel like unraveling history, and I wasn't sure if I really felt it was necessary. Was this a teenage thought brought on by my high school experience? I just couldn't stop thinking about Landon. Even when I was fighting monsters, my mind would always go back to his face and his smile. I remembered the unattended text on my phone, and pulled it from the back of my back pocket and reread his last text.

Landon: Hey! Movies tomorrow with me? :)
It is Friday so no hw. plz Bryn plz.

I thought for a second. I am in the middle of fighting for my life, and all I can think about is wanting to go see a movie with a boy! Something was going terribly wrong in my head, but I found myself with an overwhelming desire to say yes. I turned toward Brooke and Mike. "Hey, Landon wants me to go to the movies with him. What do I do?" They looked at each other and smiled.

"We will come with you! Then if some evil monster launches an attack on you, we will be there to help." Brooke smiled at her great idea.

"Yes, but that isn't my only problem. Zeus will know what I am up to, and he will not be pleased."

"I still don't get why you are so scared of him," Mike turned towards me as he spoke.

"Well he's my father, but then again he's a lot of people's father. He has had more children than you can count, and he doesn't care about any of them. Their lives mean nothing to him, and he would kill them without a second thought if they got on his wrong side. He kills anyone who dares to defy him. The Olympian council is the only place someone can defy him with hopes of waking up the next morning. He's like one of the mortal dictators; he thrives off fear."

"Well, your father sounds lovely," laughed Brooke, "but for now put him out of your mind and just text Landon. You have a date waiting!" I laughed, uncomfortably, because I was stuck between two worlds. I texted him back.

Bryn:    Sounds great! Mike and Brooke are dating and want to come with us. Is that ok?

Landon: About time! Ha ha, sounds great. As long as I'm with u it will be great.

Bryn:    What time?

Landon: 7:30. Where should I pick u up?

Bryn:    Brooke's house.

Landon: great can't wait!
Bryn:     See you later
Landon: I hope so

I didn't know if this was a good idea or not. I deluded myself into believing that if Zeus wanted me to act like a teenager, then that's just what I was doing. But I knew better.

# Chapter Six

Brooke and I talked about our date all day during school. We texted each other during every class period. Neither of us paid any attention to what our teachers were trying to teach us. For me, it didn't really matter. I didn't have to worry about my grades since I was only there for one year, and my grades didn't count for anything. So, I had the luxury of just existing as a teenager and not worrying about grades or studying. When the day had finally finished, Brooke and I headed out to go shopping for our big night out. I joked and brought a helmet from Mike's garage, even though she knew I had really given her the bump on her head. We headed to the mall to go shopping, which was never an activity I had engaged in until my experience as a teen. I wanted to hate it, but Brooke made everything fun. We literally raided every store on the block. I found myself trying on clothes with excitement. Not only was

I learning about teenage human behavior, I was actually living it!

Brooke tried on a dress that we knew was perfect for her. We drove to Brooke's house, both of us humming along with a song we loved on the radio. I had more than butterflies in my stomach; I had a swarm of mini dragons flying around in there. I had never been on a date before, and everything seemed to be going in slow motion.

Brooke's house was huge, a giant, white two-story stone house that stretched out across a rolling lawn. Dark grey shutters were attached to each window and giant white marble pillars framed the house and porch. It looked like it had come straight off Olympus. A large Willow tree drooped over the grass, its leaves swaying across the lawn in the wind. It was like being home again.

Brooke appeared stressed as she tugged and twisted her hair in various ways trying to figure out how to wear it. She was spitting out what if's and reapplying mascara in her vanity mirror. She was just making me more stressed. I jumped out of my skin when my phone rang. It was Apollo. "One second Brooke. I need to take this," I pressed accept and then put it up to my ear. "Hey Apollo, what's up?"

"Artemis! Glad I caught you. OK, so I told all the gods what you told me. Some of them had the same experience you did. Zeus claimed to have no idea, which I found odd, but I think he is pretty mad that his plan is being interrupted. I think since Zeus and everyone else knows about the problems, we will be fine. Now everyone is on the lookout for anything odd."

"Great! So does Zeus have a plan? I mean, a new plan that won't end up with every horrible creature from the Underworld trying to kill us?" I asked with sarcasm.

"No. He doesn't think it will end badly. He knows we can fend for ourselves, though he did seem upset that we would have to act like our godly selves again. He really wants us to stay in character the entire time we are here," Apollo explained.

"Well so would I. The only time I have had to 'break character' has been to save my life," I snapped back. "So, if he thinks we are all good, I am going to go enjoy my teenage life. I have my first date ever, and I plan to enjoy it," I boasted. He sighed and took a deep breath.

"Artemis, are you sure this is a good idea? I'm not certain this is what Zeus means for you. I can't imagine he intends for you to rewrite history and break your vow against men for this experiment. If Zeus found out…well I don't think he can do anything. But, what if your hunters found out? They look up to you A. If you go through with this, it will send them a confusing message about their loyalties and obligations. Have you thought this all the way through? You have others to consider than yourself."

"Calm down, Apollo!" I laughed, "I'm going out with a guy, yes, but I'm going more as a good friend to your son's new girlfriend."

"Girlfriend?" It was way too easy to distract him.

"Yes, she saved his life from an Empusa. She's one of those mortals who can see into our world."

"Are you with her?" His voice switched into dad mode. He sounded a little excitable.

"Yes! Do you want to talk to her, Apollo?" I mocked through the phone. He laughed, but agreed. "Brooke? There is someone who wants to talk to you!" I sang, "It's my brother, Mike's Daddy!" Her face went completely white.

"Ok." She just managed to choke out. I handed her the phone, but I really wanted to hear this so I put it on speakerphone. "Hello, sir. My name is Brooke," she said in an uncharacteristically flat tone.

"Hi, Brooke. You can call me Apollo. So, I hear you saved my son? Wow, and you're a mortal! I think that's totally awesome!" My brother sounded more like a teenager than Mike did.

"Th-thank you, Apollo," Brooke uttered.

"Well maybe I will come down and meet you sometime. Can you hand the phone back to my sister now?" He asked. Brooke handed the phone back to me.

"Hey, Apollo. She knows you are the real Apollo, and she knows I'm Artemis. I know we were supposed to keep our identities a secret, but it was a little difficult to do when fighting monsters from the Underworld. Anyway, thanks for giving me the update. I will carry on. Please let me know if you hear anything different. Bye! Love you."

"Love you, too. Call me after your date, and tell me how it goes. You're flirting with disaster here A. We weren't supposed to reveal ourselves to anyone. And you swore eternally to never date. This is going to be a problem; I can feel it."

"Thank you master of prophesies." I snapped my phone shut. He was my brother not my dad. I looked over to see Brooke still shaking.

"I know. It's not a big deal to talk to your boyfriend's dad, but he's a god! I probably sounded like a loser on the phone." Brooke complained to me.

"Chill, Brooke. Apollo is the biggest loser on the planet. Besides, he's the god of the sun, not war! That's Ares. Well, he is also the God of medicine, music, prophecies, poetry, and archery. That over achiever. The worst thing he would do is play the guitar and rhyme your fate in your face. It's not exactly enjoyable, but you'll live." I laughed. She seemed to relax a little.

"He seemed nice," she said quietly, almost speaking to herself.

"He is like a puppy dog." I mocked his big happy grin, and Brooke smiled. A horn honked outside, and we both flinched. "Are you ready?" I whispered. She nodded, and we ran to the front door. Outside, Mike and Landon were each standing in front of their own cars. I guess we would be riding separately.

"Bryn!" Mike called while walking over to give me a hug. He lifted me up and spun me around. He obviously wanted to make some kind of a point in front of Landon. Poor guy. Landon had no idea what we had experienced since we last saw him. Mike walked over to Brooke and gave her a kiss. She blushed and fell into his arms. Landon walked toward me while glaring at Mike. "Chill, Landon. We are related. I can hug her all I want."

"Related?" he asked confused.

"Yes, we are first cousins," he lied. Landon looked relived, and then he turned toward me.

"Really? Cousins? I was thinking y'all were, um, never mind. Hey, Bryn." His face erupted into a huge smile, and he pulled me into his arms. His hug was more romantic than Mike's spin. I hadn't ever really felt the difference between the touches of a human before. But now I knew there was a huge difference. "Are you ready to go?" he asked. I nodded, and he took my hand and led me to his car. It was black and tricked out in a way that you assumed it definitely belonged to a guy. I don't think many girls would do that to a car. Anyway, he opened my door and helped me inside. "So, Bryn. I don't really know that much about you, although I feel like I've known you forever," he said as he fired up the engine.

"What do you want to know?" I smiled.

"Let's see. Do you play any sports?" he asked, like he was trying to think of something to ask.

"I'm an archer. I also hunt." I wasn't lying. It was the complete truth. I just left out a few minor details and things like prey.

"Wow, that's cool. I have hunted before. That's awesome. A girl who likes to hunt! We should go together sometime." he said. Um...I think my hunting is a little different than his. It might freak him out if we went hunting monsters. Shooting a defenseless deer was a little different than a giant monster who is trying to rip you apart.

"That sounds great." I would just have to cancel later. "So what else do you want to know?" I asked.

"What is your favorite animal?" he asked. Weird question, I thought. Who cares what animal someone likes? "Deer," I answered. That probably wasn't accurate, but I don't think he really cared. I think he was trying to make conversation, and I was happy to answer.

"Favorite color?" he asked. Another stupid question, I thought. Is he going somewhere with this? "Silver," I replied. He looked at me as if my answer was weird. Ask a weird question, get a weird answer. His questions stopped, and he just stared at me every chance he could get. I smiled and squirmed uncomfortably in the seat of his car. I wasn't sure whether to be flattered or freaked out. I was a little of both.

We drove in silence for the rest of the ride, and I pretended to hum along to the songs on the radio. When we reached the theater, we met back up with Mike and Brooke. I was relieved to see her as it took the pressure off of Landon and me. Landon and Mike started talking about cars and how fast they could drive. Brooke was busy getting excited about the movie, some vampire flick she had been waiting to see. We walked into the dark movie theater, and I suddenly wished that I had brought a jacket. I wasn't sure if it was my nerves or the temperature, but I suddenly had the chills.

I accidentally mumbled a word in ancient Greek, and everyone looked at me awkwardly. I pretended to look for something in my purse. What was I going to do? I felt uncomfortable and confused. I felt overwhelmed by these feelings. I had never felt this feeling before. Was it guilt? Fear? These were not feelings I was accustomed to having.

We took our seats just as the movie started. Two beautiful actors strutted on screen flashing brilliant white teeth and flipping their silky hair. They looked like gods to me. I was beginning to enjoy the movie when Landon made his move. He carefully slid his arm around me. My heart raced. With his arm around my shoulder it was impossible for me to focus on the movie. He made everything impossible for me. I tried my best to pay attention to the characters on screen. I could feel Landon looking at me. He gently pulled his arm around my shoulder and leaned over to look at me. I cocked my face up to stare into his amazing blue eyes. Big mistake. He smiled, and then he leaned down towards my face. The kiss was coming. I had no idea what to do. The stakes were too high. I couldn't throw everything away like this. I started leaning in. I wanted to kiss him. The desire almost overcame me, but I pulled away at the last second. His lips awkwardly brushed against my ear as I turned away and bolted out of my seat toward the nearest exit.

I sat with my back to the wall in the empty hallway. My hands cupped my face, and I knew I was seriously freaking out. Then I felt a hand on my shoulder. I jerked my head up to see who it was who dared to interrupt my sadness. It was Landon, his face filled with concern. I was pleased to see he wasn't mad or sad, just worried about me. "Bryn?" he whispered sitting next to me and grabbing my hand. "I'm sorry if I upset you. I don't want to force you to do anything you're not comfortable with." I flinched. "Please Bryn just tell me why you ran away." His voice sounded on the verge of tears.

"I want to kiss you, Landon. I just can't. You wouldn't understand. I'm different. I'm sorry, this will never make any sense to you," I explained.

"Are you dating someone back in D.C.?" he asked, with no trace of anger in his voice.

"No. I have never had a boyfriend before. I can't have one. You would not understand." My voice trailed off.

"Is it your parents? I can talk to them. I'm really good with parents." He smiled enthusiastically as he explained himself. I smiled. Of course it had nothing to do with my parents. Zeus was technically my dad, so I guess it did have something to do with my parents, but nothing Landon's charms were going to resolve.

"No, it's not my parents," I said. By this time Brooke and Mike were standing in front of us. Mike reached down and pulled me up.

"Hey Landon, it looks like this is really bad timing, but something has come up. I have to take Bryn with me," Mike ordered. He grabbed my hand with a slight jerk and pulled me up off the floor. "Sorry, dude. You are just going to have to trust us. We should go," he said as he grabbed my hand and pulled me down the hall. I turned around to see Landon slumped on the floor. He watched us leave with a very sad and confused expression on his gorgeous face.

# CHAPTER SEVEN

I sat in the back of Mike's car as he drove down the dark highway back to his house. I stared out the window into the darkness. I could not think. I just wanted to get out of here. Then suddenly Mike jerked the car to a stop, and I looked up. He had pulled over to a small store by the side of the road. "Brooke," Mike whispered pulling out his wallet and handing it to her. "Will you go get us some snacks and drinks and whatever else you want. I need to talk to Bryn." She nodded and rushed out of the car. He cut the ignition of the car and climbed into the back seat with me. He pulled my face up so I was looking into his eyes. "Bryn, are you ok?" He stared hard into my face trying to understand my expression.

"Why am I kidding myself; I'm not human. Just because I'm pretending to be, does not mean I can change the rules I have followed for thousands of years before this. I'm crazy about him, but that does not change anything." Tears slowly dripped from my eyes, leaving streaks down my face.

"One, you're going to kill me with those tears. I can't bear to see you cry." He joked but my mouth stayed in its hard frown. "Two, you need to chill. Zeus wanted you to become absolutely human for a year. So, do it! Fall in love; fail some tests; go to parties; have fun. You're not Artemis right now; you're Bryn, a 17-year-old mortal. Even if Hades is trying to kill you, you still have to live this life Zeus has ordered for you. I have heard stories about you and my dad my whole life. For once in your very long life do what Zeus asks you to. If you break some rules in the process, that's on him not you. Most normal senior girls would not run out of a movie when a guy tries to kiss them. For some reason Zeus wants you to experience this, so experience it." His words seemed to make some sense in a strange way.

"I understand where you are coming from, but I don't know if it's that easy." I moaned. I knew I had some serious soul searching to do. If I chose to give-in to this human emotion, I would change the course of my godly life, and the lives of my huntresses for eternity. That was too big a decision to make at a movie theater with the first boy I liked, even if he was too beautiful to believe. Life would be so much easier if I could just act impulsively like a normal teenager. But I couldn't, and I knew it.

"It can be that easy," Mike argued. "I have heard stories my whole life about how strong you are. You're Artemis. You can do anything!" He exclaimed, and I recoiled back into the seat. He saw that and sighed.

"Bryn, talk to Apollo about it tonight and then decide. He seems to know a lot. Try to think about it. Ok?" I nodded. He sighed. Just then Brooke exited the store with two small, white plastic bags in her hands. She stayed there until Mike got out of the car to tell her what we had talked about and lead her back to the passenger seat. She passed me back a bag of mini cookies and a bottle of root beer. My eyes lit up, and she smiled.

"See Mike, the way to get Bryn happy is with sugar." I laughed because she was right. She was the only one who knew that. I ripped open the bag and jammed a mini Oreo into my mouth. The taste soothed me. I definitely had the hunger of a teenager, which was another first for me. Although I did not technically need food, it still tasted good.

Mike dropped Brooke off at her house, but went in first to introduce himself to her parents. I took that opportunity to call Apollo. "Hey," I whispered when he answered. By then I was in control of my emotions and could talk.

"So, it's too early for the date to have ended. How awful was it?" He knew something bad would happen, and this was his subtle way of saying 'I told you so'.

"He tried to kiss me."

"So?"

"I think, I might really have a problem here. I know I have only known him for a few weeks, but the way I feel, it's strange. It's not…I don't know. I can't date. Ever. I swore that I wouldn't. Anyway, I'm like thousands of years old, and he is 17. I could get arrested down here. I'm in big trouble." I realized I was rambling. The words were pouring out of my mouth. "Your son says I should just be human and go with it. Blame it on Zeus."

"So, let me get this straight. In the few weeks you have been a mortal, you have been ferociously attacked by three separate monsters from the Underworld, but your biggest concern is whether or not you should kiss this kid? Really, Art? This isn't like you. Don't lose your head over this."

"Ok then, what do I do"?

"About the boy, or our imminent danger of being obliterated by beasts from another world? The boy I assume. Ok, just go out with him. When it's time to become a goddess again, you can talk to Zeus about the rule."

"Thanks, Apollo. Sorry, I think being a teenage girl is wreaking havoc on my emotions. I have to go. Love you. Bye."

I hung up the phone, just as Brooke was walking Mike out to the car. He kissed her and then stepped into the car and waved until we were out of site. "I called Apollo, and he agrees with you." He just nodded. The good thing about Mike was he did not pry. I was very thankful. He just held my hand and hummed to the radio. When we got home I collapsed on the couch and wanted an uncharacteristic nap. Mike had other ideas. He popped popcorn and pulled out about ten board games. Then he opened up the bags of snacks Brooke had purchased. When he opened the bag, he dumped its contents on to the floor. We both laughed at the sight. The bag was filled with five bags of mini Oreos and six bottles of root beer.

"So we are going to play board games. It helps me when I'm sad." It sounded silly, but I was willing to give it a try. We played Mousetrap, which is harder to set up than it is to play, and we were starting a game of Monopoly. I was enjoying beating my nephew and was just about to buy the third railroad when my phone rang. I saw it was Landon. Mike nodded and walked away into the backyard to give me some space to talk. I answered but just stayed silent as Landon's voice filled my ear.

"Bryn?" I could tell that he was still as confused now as he was when we left him in the theater.

"Hey, Landon. I'm sorry about today, but if you could give me another chance," my voice broke off at the end. I had no idea what to ask of him.

"I understand…kind of. I just want to know, why."

"It's very complicated. I don't know where to start to explain."

"This cousin story of yours. Is that really true? I just talked to Brooke, and she told me you are hanging out with Mike right now. Really? You bailed on me to go hang out with Mike?" he asked accusingly.

"No, I swear that is completely true. He is my family and understands my situation. I'm sorry."

"So, if you like me, why would you rather hang out with your cousin? I don't mean to judge, but that seems a little odd to me. I guess I just don't get it. I'm trying Bryn, but it doesn't make a lot of sense."

"I want to make it up to you. I can't explain it all, because it doesn't all make sense. You're right. But, can we give it one more try?" I hoped he would say yes.

"Sure. Will you go to dinner with me tomorrow night at the Cove, and we can talk and maybe this time you don't bring any additional family members? Just me and you."

"Sounds great. I will see you tomorrow." I hung up the phone.

*What the hell am I getting myself into?* I tried not to think about it as Mike and I continued our game night. I have to say it worked! We played Clue, Life, and Battleship. I had to learn the rules of all the games before we even started. It was fun and exhausting. After a few games, Mike excused himself to go call Brooke. I pulled out my phone and ignored the text I had gotten from Brooke. I would call her later. I texted Apollo.

> Artemis: Going to go out with Landon. If Zeus does not like it well, oh well Anything else happening?
>
> Apollo: Good for U Art! Have fun. Relax. Afraid things are not going to stay EZ for long.

Then I saw I had four texts from Brooke.

> Brooke: Hey, how are you doing?
> Brooke: Bryn?
> Brooke: Mike just called. Ur going out with Landon tomorrow?
> Brooke: BRYN!!!!!!

I decided I would call her tomorrow; right now, I had other things I had to do.

At Olympus, every night I would fly my chariot around the world to usher the moon across the sky.

As I stared outside and saw the moon rising over the Texas sky, I wondered how the moon was put into place without me there. Apollo would pull the sun across the sky at dawn, and I was pretty sure he wasn't doing that during his high school experience either. I wondered how much of my life Zeus actually controlled. I was sure I knew a lot less about myself than I had previously thought. The night was clear and every star shone perfectly. I longed to feel my goddess form, so I snuck out to hunt. I needed to face a monster or hellhound to unleash my godly powers again.

When I got home, it was almost morning, and I walked in to see Mike crashed on the couch. I didn't want him to realize I had been out hunting all night, so I found my way to the kitchen to make breakfast. I knew bacon and eggs would be a good distraction when he awoke. When the bacon started to sizzle, Mike woke up. "Bryn! You didn't have to make me breakfast! What time did you go to bed last night?" he asked as he managed his way into the kitchen.

"Oh, I don't think it was too late," I winked, "and I didn't make it for you, I made it for us. Wake up your mom, and we can all have breakfast together." It was great to spend time with Mike's mom. I never knew her, and it was weird to imagine my brother with her. She told us stories about meeting Apollo and Mike as a baby. These were the moments I enjoyed during my human experience, comfy pajamas on the sofa, drinking coffee, and listening to stories with my family. That was something I could appreciate for a long time, and I began to appreciate Zeus for giving me this experience.

I was learning, loving, and experiencing life in a way I had never done before. I found appreciation in this experience, which was a good feeling.

Throughout breakfast I ignored the constant text tone blowing up on my phone. When I finally checked it, I saw that Brooke had texted me twelve times and called me twice. It was obviously necessary to spend some time with my needy friend. I thanked Mike and Holly for the food before making my way to Brooke's house.

As I pulled up into her driveway, Brooke was already waiting for me on the front porch.

"Bryn, I know you're a goddess and all, but that does not give you authority to ignore you best friend." She smiled. As Artemis I would have never let somebody speak to me like that, but I was becoming more accustomed to the mortals challenging me.

"I'm sorry Brooke. You have had seventeen years to adjust to becoming a teenager. I have had a few weeks, and it's about to kill me." We rushed past her parents and up to her bedroom. "I didn't even get a chance to say hi to your parents." I sat on her bed and fake pouted. She grabbed my arm and screeched at me.

"So I have to find out, through Mike, you are giving Landon a second chance?" she squealed in frustration.

"Brooke, chill. I think they can hear you on Olympus! But yes, I am going to completely give into being human. Then Zeus can't complain. It was his idea in the first place." Brooke's face got really thoughtful as she considered this information. Then she nodded, giving me the signal that she understood, and I had her approval. "When are y'all going out?" she asked. When I told her it was tonight, her face lit up with pure joy.

"Whoa! Oh my god! What are you going to wear? Where are you going?" I laughed. Of course Brooke would only care about that. She made forgetting about the hard stuff very easy.

"The Cove. I have no clue what I'm wearing, that's why I am here." Brooke just smiled and pulled me in to her huge walk-in closet. It was filled to the brim with clothes. It made me wonder why she ever went shopping with this many clothes already in her closet. Some of the clothes were edgy, others more classic. The farther back you went you could see the fads that Brooke had gone through in the last 5 years.

The Cove was a restaurant with a large outdoor courtyard where a band would play while diners ate their dinner. It would be a perfect place to relax and really get to know Landon better. I had so many questions I wanted to ask him. I really just wanted to be with him and enjoy his company. Brooke broke my daydream by putting a small white cotton dress on my lap for consideration. We both shook our heads.

"Too nice." I dictated, and the dress went back in its proper place. She pulled a fitted tank top and mini skirt. I fake gagged. "You should know me better than that," we both laughed and the awful outfit went back into the dark where it belonged. I'm not a fan of skirts. You can hunt in a dress but in a skirt you might as well tie my legs together with a cable. The next outfit was a pair of denim shorts with roses on them and a light pink t-shirt.

"That will work I guess." I nodded to the clothes she held in her hands.

"Perfect." Brooke said as if complimenting her choice. Then she threw the outfit at me. "Now get dressed, and I will do your hair and makeup. We really need to work on your sense of style."

"Uh, Brooke, it's only like noon. I don't think I need to get ready quite yet," I reminded her.

"You're right; that will give me plenty of time to do your nails, and a facial." She carried on, but I stopped listening. I went where she told me to and posed for her to be my personal fashion and beauty assistant. All I could think about was how much I wanted to be with Landon, without any chaperones this time. I hoped the night would be peaceful and special. I daydreamed about it all day.

After hours of preparation, her work was done. "You look beautiful," she said as she admired me, her creation. I looked in the mirror, and I could barely recognize myself. Not bad, Brooke. You do good work, I thought. I texted Landon to make sure he knew to pick me up at Brooke's house. I was hoping he would come soon, because Brooke's touch-ups on my hair were making me crazy nervous.

Soon there was a soft knock at the door, and I walked slowly down the stairs. There was Landon standing on the front porch looking more gorgeous than he was in my daydreams. His eyes widened when he saw me coming down the staircase. Before I could step my feet on the marble floor Brooke was already at the door. She whipped open the large white doors and ushered

Landon into the foyer. He smiled and pulled me into a long hug and kissed the top of my head. I sighed; I was really going to do this.

"Easy there guys, this is a family show. Let's keep it PG," Brooke smiled. "Now, I want you home before midnight," Brooke joked. She pried me from Landon's arms and kissed my cheeks. She ran up the stairs giggling. "Be good kids."

"Are you ready to go, Bryn?" He did not even give me time to answer. He grabbed my hand and whisked me out the house and into his car. When we got in the car he started blasting some rap music and jumping up and down in his seat.

"Well aren't we hyper today?" I laughed. He just grabbed my hand. I leaned back in my seat listening to the song blasting from the stereo, making the car shake. He seemed to be as happy to be with me as I was to be with him. This was a feeling I would never forget. When we got to the restaurant, Landon walked to my car door and opened it for me. He drew his arm back to display the dusty road as if it was the red carpet.

"Here you are, Madam. I hope you enjoyed your ride." Landon said in a mock British accent.

"Why, thank you, my good man!" We walked into the restaurant already laughing. Not a bad start to our date. A small country band was playing loudly inside the restaurant. We decided to take one of the picnic tables outside. We both ordered burgers and sweet potato fries. We talked about everything. We shared funny stories that had happened to us. Most of them I had to tweak a little, so I would not give away the fact that I was a goddess. Like the one time that I had first used the demi-gods portal to Olympus in the White House, and I had accidentally opened the door to the President dancing to a Lady Gaga song with his daughter. I changed the story enough to keep it interesting and left Landon thinking I had been taking a tour of the White House with my former high school and just happened upon the room.

As we were talking and laughing, we turned to see that a different waiter appeared at our table. I gasped. The 'waiter' was an old lady with giant, leathery wings and claws the size of my face. The creature who stood before me was one of the three Furies or Erinyes. There were three of these old hags flying around the world making everyone's life horrible. When Kronos, who was the lord of everything before Zeus overthrew him, killed his father, he threw Uranus's dead body into the ocean. Out of this rose Aphrodite and the three Erinyes. They were the goddesses of vengeance. In some depictions they were shown as beautiful young women with giant black wings, but really they looked like something that had been buried and then dragged through Hell.

Of course to everyone else she probably just looked like an old woman. She smiled at me showing me her ugly yellow fangs. Then she looked over to Landon.

"I hope you are enjoying everything. Would you mind if I borrowed Artemis for just a moment?" I shot her a dirty look. She can't call me that name in front of mortals! Was she insane? Well yes she probably was. I smiled at Landon and shot him an I'm-super-sorry look. Then, I walked behind her and pulled out the emergency sword that I kept in my purse, a necessary precaution for the hunting goddess. I never know who or what I am going to run into, and my purse was a magical gift from Hephaestus that shrunk anything that went inside it. You really can't imagine how many weapons I have hidden in my sporty, stylish bag. As we walked around back of the restaurant, I raised the sword to strike it through her head. She side-stepped my swipe and caught the side of my sword. Dammit. That's why I use arrows.

"Calm down, you spoiled brat. I come in peace to warn you of what's to come. You need to keep an eye out for your loved ones. They are in grave danger." She warned.

"Why are you telling me this? What do you care if my loved ones live or die?"

"I don't. If it was my choice I would kill them all myself. I'm here on Hades' orders. You're lucky he sent me for you; others might have attacked you as their warning."

"Thanks for your concern about my safety, but I don't trust you. I don't believe you are here on a mission of mercy from Hades to give me fair warning."

"You must believe…"

Whatever she was going to say was cut off. I blocked the hidden sword she was about to plunge into me, twisted it out of her claws and thrust it into her stomach. As her corpse was falling to the ground, I waved it away to the Underworld. I stuffed my own sword in my purse and returned to the table where Landon was sitting. I looked around to ensure no one had seen us. Although the Erinye was gone, her words still rung in my head. What had she been talking about? They were not known to lie, being the goddesses of vengeance; they wanted to tell the truth; it would hurt more.

"Hey! Who was that? Someone from D.C? She called you Artemis, and isn't that what your old friends called you?" Wow I had almost forgotten about that lie.

"Yes, she's an old friend. It was good to see her. So where were we?" I winced. I realized we wouldn't be getting our dinner as I had just killed our waitress. So, I pretended not to notice how long it was taking. Landon became visibly upset that no one was helping us. Finally, he stopped another waiter who promised to find our server. Not likely, I thought. After an agonizing wait, the waiter reappeared and told us it seemed our waitress had disappeared, but he would help us. I wanted to tell him that not only did she disappear but also she had been banished to the Underworld. I decided to just smile.

We continued our meal. I was actually able to relax and enjoy the rest of our night together. As we made our way out to his car, he opened my door like a proper gentleman. When I sat down, I turned toward him, my feet dangling out of the car. I started kicking up the dust on the road. Landon leaned into the car to kiss me. This time, I did not turn away. I let his lips press against mine. It was like someone had set-off a fireworks display in my mind. I was filled with a burst of happiness. Three seconds later he pulled away. My heart dropped from its place on cloud nine. Did he have to stop so soon? I let out a small giggle, which was completely odd. I almost never giggled.

"Now was that so bad?" I did not want to answer his I-told-you-so-question. So instead I pulled his head back into mine and pressed my lips into his. I could stay there forever. After about thirty seconds of pure bliss, he laughed and pulled away. "I'm going to get drunk from kissing you, and then how will I drive?"

"Yes, please. No drunk drivers." I sighed as he closed the door and got into the driver's seat. He grabbed my hand and drove back to Brooke's house. I had so much to tell her! My heart was about to explode with love for the boy holding my hand. She had to know everything. As we pulled up to the house, Landon sighed. He put his face in my hair.

"Do you have to go?" He mumbled into my hair.

"No, I don't, but I probably should." These were definitely confusing teenager thoughts and feelings. I did not want to leave. I knew I shouldn't stay. I leaned up and kissed him again. I was pure Bryn at this moment. If Artemis was inside me, I couldn't hear her or feel her. And I was glad.

"I'll call you later." Landon promised. I smiled. He squeezed my hand, and then I walked on air into Brooke's house. I greeted Brooke's parents and then walked upstairs to tell Brooke what had happened. I couldn't wait to share every detail with my best friend. I opened the door into her soft, pink room. It was still and quiet. Her bed was unmade; her makeup was strewn on the floor, exactly how I had left it three hours ago. On her bed lay a piece of ivory paper folded in half. I opened it and almost collapsed to the floor. My knees went weak, and I steadied myself on Brooke's bed. What had I done? The note contained six words that scared me more than any monster I had ever faced.

I told you to be careful.

# Chapter Eight

He took Brooke. Hades took Brooke. If I could get my hands on him right now, I swear I would rip his head off! Just on cue, the air to the side of me shimmered slightly. Then, Hades stood beside me in all his hellish glory. Flames, heat, and demons surrounded him. I grabbed at him, but my hand just passed through him. His image was there, but his body was not. Was I dreaming? Was he really there? I could see him, and I could feel the heat of his presence. But, I could not feel him. Then, he began to speak. "Artemis, darling! How long has it been?" He spoke as if we were actually friends, "Far too long!"

"Hmm... I think it has not been long enough. Now tell me, why did you send your stupid little monsters after me when you could have come and challenged me yourself?" I asked. Hades chuckled darkly.

"Well. It seems to me that you are missing somebody here." His voice sounded smug. A growl ripped through my throat.

"I suggest you let her go before I come down there and rip your heart out. Oh wait, you don't have a heart! I swear I will find you and drown you in the river Styx!"

"Oh my darling niece, you seem to have forgotten the river Styx is in the Underworld, so it is under my control. If you would like, I can dip your friend in and see if she's strong enough to survive. If she does, she could be like Achilles! If she doesn't, she will disintegrate forever." He laughed his evil laugh. The river Styx would disintegrate you if you just stepped into it. A few demigods could force their will to keep them alive and make them invincible. Achilles' heel was not dipped into the river, so it remains his one vulnerable spot. We both knew that as a mortal Brooke would die an immediate death. "Let's hope she doesn't happen to slip into the river while she is waiting for you." He sneered.

"If you take her one step towards that damned river, I will put an arrow through your vile head."

"Oh Artemis, you always were a dramatic one. Now let's talk for a second. You see, I don't want to kill this girl. I want to set her free. All she does is talk; she never shuts up! It is annoying the hell out of me. Literally! So here's the thing. You have two days to think it over. If you come and surrender yourself to me, then I will set your annoying friend free. It's as simple as that. If you don't, she dies."

"I already know my choice. Take me, and set her free."

"I said two days," his voiced boomed. "You and your little boyfriend seem to be having so much fun. I would hate to cut your visit short. If you come to me, I swear on the river Styx I will release her. But if you come with anyone else, I will kill her. The choice is yours." I knew he meant what he said. When a god swears on the Styx, they are bound by the river to follow the commitment. It's an unbreakable promise.

"See you on Sunday," I muttered. He flashed me a smile, and then was gone. "Have fun with your human boy!" He howled as he disappeared. I collapsed on the floor again, and for the second time in my life started to cry. I was becoming more human every day.

Now I needed a plan so Brooke's parents would not notice that she was gone and wouldn't be back until Sunday, if everything went well.

The idea came to me. I walked downstairs and told her parents goodbye and drove off. I parked the car a block down the road and ran back to Brooke's house. As a god, I can appear or reappear where I am needed. I am not bound by walls or time, but as part of my contract with Zeus, I was supposed to follow the same physical laws that humans were bound to, like gravity. I was pretty sure, I was not supposed to use my power of physical transportation, but I am pretty sure I wasn't supposed to kiss Landon either. So I decided to throw all caution to the wind and appear in Brooke's room, rather than try to scale the walls of her colossal home!

Once I was back in her room, I transformed myself to look exactly like Brooke. I packed a small bag of her clothes, her phone and makeup. Then I walked back downstairs and into the living room where her parents were sitting. I remembered what Brooke said about her dad being a pushover, so I directed my question to him. "Hey, dad?" He turned his head toward me and looked lovingly into my eyes.

"Hi sweetie! What's up?"

"Well, Bryn is having some guy drama. She is really upset by all of it. I feel like she really needs me right now. I was thinking maybe I could go stay with her for the weekend to help her out. She really needs me." As I spoke, I contorted the veil over his mind so that he would want to say yes, just in case.

"Of course. You're so thoughtful with your friends." Success!

"Thank you! I will be back Sunday. I love y'all. Call me if you need me. I will keep my phone on." I kissed them both on the head and ran out the door. I couldn't believe I just lied to Brooke's parents. What was I becoming in this teenaged mind of mine?

I rushed to the car and drove away as quickly as the car would drive. Mike needed to know what was happening. I thought of calling him, but I knew how upset he would be. I had to be there to help him when I delivered the news that his girlfriend had been literally banished to Hell by Hades. That wasn't a conversation for the phone.

I drove up to his house and jumped out of the car. I ran to the front door and thrust it open in a mad dash to find Mike. He was standing in the kitchen and looked surprised and almost too happy to see me. He grabbed me in his arms and then started to lean down. What the heck? Was he trying to kiss me? Then I realized I still looked like Brooke! I hadn't changed my form back to Bryn. He leaned down and pressed his lips to mine, and I shoved him off me.

"Brooke, what's wrong?" He sounded hurt. I changed my form back into Bryn, and he gasped. "What the hell, man? What are you doing? Why did you just look like Brooke?"

"Hades took Brooke! He wants to get to me, so he took Brooke!" My words came out harsh, not the gentle message I was planning to deliver. The awkward nephew kiss threw me off. The look on Mike's face was heartbreaking.

I told him all that happened on my date with Landon and the visit I had gotten from the Erinye. I explained that Brooke was gone when I returned. I showed him the note I had kept in my pocket. I told him about my talk with the god of the Underworld and how I was going turn myself in for her. He just sat there shocked, tears rolling down his cheeks. "I'm going to rip Hades' head off." Wow, I thought. We think alike! "There has to be a way to get Brooke back without turning yourself in. Why does he have to pick the two most important people in my life?" He asked painfully. I felt sorry for Mike. He was clearly distraught. He was pacing across the room, pounding his fist into his other hand.

"We need to be calm and think, Mike. We are dealing with one of the most powerful gods of all times. He has powers you can't imagine. He is probably watching us right now. As gods, we learned about his Helmet of Darkness. It looks like a hat, and when he wears it he becomes invisible. It's completely undetectable, kind of like a cold wind that can go everywhere. You can't see him or touch him but it gets cold. His name means *The Unseen*. He can't be tricked."

"I will not let you turn yourself in. We have to figure something out." Mike blurted at me. I knew I needed to be calm but strong. I needed to remember what I was learning about teenage humans and not behave like one. Mike was a demigod, which means he was half human. His ego and his anger would get in the way of his ability to make a good decision here.

"This is not your fight," I told him. "I need you to listen and support me in this."

"Yes, it is my fight." He demanded, spewing spit and anger at me. "You're not doing this!" He demanded.

"How are you going stop me?" I asked.

"What if we get Apollo to help us get Brooke back?"

"The second we do, he will kill her."

"There has to be a way."

"Well there is not!" I demanded.

"I'm calling Apollo."

"You do, and I will kill you. This is my fight. I might need your help, but you will not do one thing without me. You have no idea what you are dealing with." I stormed out of the house and got into my car.

I had no idea where I was going, but I needed to get there soon. I needed to get away from the trappings of the human condition Zeus had demanded of me. I needed to retreat, to return to Artemis. I am the goddess of the hunt. I needed to become my true self to solve this. There was no way for me to do what I needed to do as Bryn. The road was dark, and the air that came through my window was hot. It flushed my cheeks, and it cleared my mind. My phone started to ring, so I pulled over on the side of the road. Landon was calling. I sighed and pressed decline. I'm sorry Landon, but this was not the time. I floored the gas and flew down the open road. I knew I was not stopping anytime soon.

By the time the sun rose, I had been sitting in a small 24/7 diner in Austin, Texas for seven hours. I had consumed ten cups of pure, black coffee. For gods this was fine. It had no physical effect on me, though the lady at the counter was giving me a very concerned look. "Rough night?" She asked in a sweet, southern accent. I just nodded. Even after ten cups of coffee, I was still too tired to talk. I guess the lady could read my expression and started to brew another cup. "Breakfast?" The lady asked gently. I just nodded. "I'll bring you something good." She smiled, poured more coffee into my cup, and walked to the kitchen. I pulled out my phone to see three missed calls from Landon, five from Mike and a text from Apollo. I looked at Apollo's text first knowing it would be the easiest to handle.

Apollo: Bryn, Mike called. Plz call me. Hades hasn't only taken Brooke. He took my daughter. Need ur help. Call me.

I answered Apollo with a text of desperation.

Bryn:     I'm here. Please help. Be on the
          lookout. What should we do?
Apollo:   Just wait. Hades won't do anything for
          2 days. Need to think. Keep ur phone
          close by.
Bryn:     Thanks.

I felt bad for Mike. He had not done anything wrong. I called him, and he picked up on the first ring, which made me smile. "Bryn thank God! Are you ok? Where are you? I know you're a goddess or whatever, but you just can't bail on me like that. Not ok. I have been worried sick. I haven't been able to sleep. I called Apollo. Y'all are so much alike sometimes. He actually agrees with you. Wait...where are you?" I laughed out loud. That boy could talk for hours.

"Austin. I think I'm going to stay here tonight. I will head back tomorrow. I need some time to think, and I don't want to be close to anyone I care about right now. If Hades wants to send anyone for me, I am not going to risk anyone else's life," I said as tears welled up in my eyes.

"Bryn, I don't like this. You are alone out there. I can't lose you both." His voice cut-off at the end. "I should have been there. I should have stopped Hades from taking her. I could have—"This time I cut him off.

"Mike, you could not have stopped him. He would have killed you, and you have not lost her. I'm going to get her back. I love you, Mike. I'll talk to you later." I quickly hung up before he could respond. The deep pain in his voice was too much for me to handle. I called Landon next. He did not pick up, so I decided I would leave him a message. "Hey." I searched for what to say next. I hated leaving voicemails. I felt like anything I said would sound like empty lies. But, I had to say something. "I'm sorry for not answering. Something came up with Brooke, and I had to rush up to Austin. I will be back on Sunday or Monday. Don't miss me too much." I hung up. I knew my voice lacked its usual enthusiasm, but I couldn't find the strength to fake the story and the emotion.

I wondered what he would think when he heard it. As I was deep in thought, the smell of eggs, bacon, and a stack of pancakes overwhelmed me. The sweet Southern waitress patted my back as she put the plate in front of me. As I thanked her, she simply smiled and nodded. She went in the kitchen again and came out with some syrup. I dug into the best breakfast I had ever had. I'm not sure how many breakfasts I had actually ever eaten, but I was sure this one was the best. Food did comfort me at times, and I knew I needed some comfort now. I paid the waitress and walked out of the diner. I left my car behind and started to walk. I walked past the giant convention center, where teenaged girls, dressed for some sporting event, poured in. I walked by a couple of local restaurants and finally found myself standing in front of a small motel where I would stay the night. I booked room 16A, and as soon as I sat on the bed, I crashed. Sleep wasn't something I generally required, but I could sleep to restore myself. I knew I needed all the energy I could find, so I let myself go into a dreamless sleep.

I woke up at 8:45 P.M, which means I had literally slept the entire day. I should not need sleep. I didn't even know I could sleep a full 12 hours. I wrapped myself in a robe and stumbled to the shower. The water washed over me and brought me back to life. I turned the nozzle as hot it would go until the water was scalding. My skin turned a bright shade of pink. After ten minutes of being lost in my thoughts, I climbed out of the shower and put my clothes back on. I knew it was time to go; I just didn't know to where. I couldn't get clarity around how I was going to save my friend.

I needed to get some fresh air. I walked into the warm Austin air. The sun had set, and the city had come alive. I could hear a concert going on down the street at Zilker Park. I drifted toward the sound of the music, but I was cut short. I walked up to someone who, to be honest, I really had no patience to deal with.

Aphrodite sat on a small table in front of a coffee shop. She had a small compact mirror in which she was reapplying her lip-gloss. As I walked closer she looked up and snapped her compact shut and stared deeply at me with a warm smile. Her long wavy chocolate brown hair fell to her shoulders and her flawless face glowed in the light of the bright Austin moon. I couldn't imagine that she was sitting out in public in her goddess form. Someone would know she was not human. She was too pretty. Sure, all goddesses are beautiful, prettier than any mortal, but Aphrodite could literally take your breath away. She was perfect in every way. It was her strength. It was her weapon. "Hello, Artemis! Don't you look lovely? Come sit with me; for I fear I have some terrible news." *Oh dear*, I thought. *Are they out of mascara again?*

"To what do I owe the honor"? I tried desperately to keep the sarcasm out of my voice, but it had been a long day, and this is not what I needed.

"Your adorable brother Apollo told me to come find you here. It's Hades. He has sent so many monsters after me; I just can't take it! Then he took one of my dear mortal friends, and I must get him back. He means everything to me. I cannot let anything happen to him. Hades is coming after all of us, Artemis. You have to do something. My powers aren't going to help in this situation. You are the goddess of the hunt, so hunt him down and make him stop. My friend, my new friend, cannot handle what will happen to him in the Underworld. He's not built like that," she gushed. This guy sounded like more than her friend to me. Aphrodite didn't just make friends.

She continued, "Hades told me that in order to get him back, I would have to give myself over to Hades and live in the Underworld! Trust me, I am willing to make some sacrifices, but I am not designed for that life. It's dark and hot and fiery —and humid. It just won't work. You have to help me Artemis." She quickly fluffed her hair for effect and then took a dainty little sip of the latte that was sitting in front of her.

"I reached out to Apollo," she explained, "because I didn't know who else could help me. He told me to find you here and for us to wait. I think he is going to contact the others to see if Hades is launching an attack on each of us. Is it true? Did Hades take one of your mortal friends, too?"

"Yes," I told her, "he took my newest, dearest human friend. Her name is Brooke, and I'm going to turn myself in on Sunday to get her back. Case closed. You can turn yourself in if you want to or not, but I have decided. Brooke didn't ask for this, and I can't have this happen to her because of me. I won't let it happen. Humidity or not, I'm going."

Aphrodite's eyes widened like she could not believe I had already made my decision that I would have chosen to save a mortal's life over my own. I don't think the thought had really ever crossed her perfect little head. She just wanted my brother and me to save her. I am pretty sure she never considered saving her friend by herself.

"Well then, I see there is nothing to discuss here since you have made your decision. I will be on my way. I may or may not see you on Sunday. Until next time dear." She stood up and strutted down the street. Heads turned as she passed. Men's mouths lay hanging open. She was definitely something to see.

I knew I should try to stop her. Apollo would be furious with me for letting her go, but there was no way I was going to convince her to stay and fight. She wasn't exactly the fighting type. I could not figure out what to do. If Hades was methodically picking us off one by one and taking the people we cared about, then he would win. Gods are designed with certain characteristics, which make them uniquely strong. I was willing to fight for Brooke, because fighting is what I do. I would naturally be up for a fight. But the other gods wouldn't. They weren't going to sacrifice themselves for a mortal. It just wouldn't happen. But if the gods had experienced their human form, if this experiment of Zeus's had actually worked, perhaps the other gods would feel differently. Maybe what I felt about Brooke wasn't my goddess spirit, but my human spirit. Maybe all of us had tapped into a part of ourselves we had never been open to before. I sat there wondering if this was part of Zeus's plan. Zeus would never do anything selfless. He was intentional and self-motivated at all times. He never cared about anything more than himself. I didn't understand. I wasn't sure whose side he was really on.

I made my way back to the hotel, trying to determine my best course of action. When I reached my room, I collapsed into my bed and quickly fell asleep. In my dream I traveled to the Underworld. Sleep is different for the gods. We don't need it, but we can go there to receive energy, messages, visions, warnings, and communication from others. A fellow god can will you to see what he or she wants you to see, and you are suddenly overcome with the urge to sleep. Sleep messages are generally ominous warnings. I was suddenly in the castle of Hades. He sat in his throne room on a large black throne adorned with jewels. Even in darkness, it sparkled. Hades was also the god of all the minerals and riches, for they were formed underground.

In his throne room were eleven shining diamond cages. Each cage held a mortal or demigod, a friend whom one of the gods had gotten close to during their time as humans. The mortals looked scared and confused. Their faces were filled with fear and frustration. The fear in their eyes was terrifying. In my dream state, I could only observe. I was confused, yet I knew exactly what was happening in front of me. Our friends were caged like animals in a dark world they never knew existed. They must have been truly terrified.

I searched the eleven cages to find Brooke. I was relieved and furious when I saw her locked inside a cage. I didn't see fear in Brooke. I could see emotion, but I couldn't tell what it was. Then I heard her call out in anger, "Hey Hades! King of the dead freaks! Want to, you know, let us out? No offense but I really don't like you, and I want to go home. And if you don't, I'm pretty sure a bunch of angry gods are going to come and kick your undead ass. You really think you can defeat eleven other gods and goddesses? Did your mom drop you on your undead head as a baby?" she hissed at him. Aaah. There it was, unbridled, teenage anger. I had felt it myself for the first time over the last few weeks. Good job, Brooke!

"Would you shut up?" Hades bellowed from his thrown. He had his fingers pressed to his temple as if his head was throbbing. "What do you not understand about surrendering? They are surrendering themselves for you. They aren't going to fight, because if they do I will kill all of you!" he exploded. Brooke rolled her eyes and let out a sarcastic sigh.

"Whatever. You're wrong, and I can't wait until they get here, which they will. I am just saying I really don't think you have thought this one all the way through, oh great one. Honestly though, do you seriously think a bunch of cages can hold gods captive? What are you going to do when you have them in these cages? Stare at them until they die of boredom? I can't wait to watch you go down even further than the Underworld," she said with a sarcastic tone in her voice. A smaller demigod boy spoke up from his cage.

"Two things. Number one, I totally agree with the annoying mortal girl, and number two, when exactly are the gods coming? I'm sick of this place, and if I don't get out soon, I'm going to kill someone. Preferably you, Hades." He harshly spat at Hades. All the other demigods muttered their agreement. One mortal started to cry. Although, I was seeing this in a dream, it was clear and real, as if I was watching it all happen in real life. I wanted to say something. I wanted to tell Brooke she was right, and I was coming. I would surrender if I had to, but I would fight if I needed to. I wanted to tell the little crying mortal girl it would be ok. I needed to say something. I started to talk, and as I spoke, my voice rang though the throne room. Cool, I thought. I can talk in these dreams.

"Hades, it's Artemis. I will be there Sunday, and you will keep your promise. Brooke, you are completely right. We will fight. The gods are uniting. And Hades, your brother Zeus has given us all a new gift. We now understand the mind of a teenage human. Just like the ones you have caged in your sick little plan here. We will all harness our human and godly strength to free them. You will fail Hades. You should let them go now, before it gets ugly."

"Artemis!" Brooke called, "you don't have to do this! I will be fine. Don't turn yourself in for me! Your life is worth more than mine." The assurance in her voice broke my heart. She was so wrong. Her precious life had affected so many others, including mine.

"Brooke dear, I will be there. I will not be the reason for your death. Now keep on making Hades miserable. It's making me very proud. I love you and will see you soon. But one last thing, Hades, just so we are clear. Brooke is completely right. You will lose." Then with that, I was gone from my own dream.

# CHAPTER NINE

I woke up Saturday morning early; at least, I think I woke up. I'm not exactly sure if I was sleeping or just thinking. But I did have a dream, so I must have had some sleep. I awoke in a cold sweat thanks to my trip to the Underworld. I got up, brushed my hair and teeth. I checked out of my room and jogged back to the small diner where I had left my car.

I floored it back to San Antonio. I was way too distracted to stop for breakfast, and I made it back in record time. I was at Mike's house by 8:30. When I opened the door Mike jumped up and swung his arms around me. He had a huge smile on his face. I'm pretty sure he thought he would never see me again.

"Bryn! Oh thank god you're OK. Don't ever storm out on me like that again. I was afraid I would lose you. Oh, wait what's wrong?" he asked.

"Last night in my dream, I visited the Underworld. He has them locked in cages. Mike, it's bad. It's even worse than I thought. If you think you're going to stop me from saving her now, you are very wrong. I will be ok. I'm a goddess; he can't kill me. I never actually die, but Brooke is mortal and her life is in the hands of a very unstable god. I have to save her." Mike's face went completely blank. I could see the fear he was trying to suppress. Tears gathered around his eyes.

"How many mortals were captured?" He asked in a pained voice, as if afraid of the answer.

"Eleven total demigods and mortals. One for every god except Hades." His face drained of color.

"So someone has been captured because of my dad?" I nodded. He collapsed on the couch behind him and let out a sigh. "Bryn, I don't like this at all." I sat next to him and put my arm around him. Tears slowly started to pour out of his eyes, sliding down his face. It shocked me, literally shocked me. He looked so much like Apollo, and he had such human emotion running through him. It was such a strange combination to witness. Though Apollo would never cry, it was like watching a younger version of him, and I could not bear to see him like this. It broke my heart. My chest tightened and I had to fight back the tears that were brimming in my eyes. My stomach felt as if it were sinking in to the depths of the ocean. It was a whole new sensation to me, all dark and sad but at the same time tinted with a sort of underlying rage. I had lived through the classic clash of the gods fighting the Titans, the time when we almost lost everything. At that time, I had felt nothing. The time I was betrayed by my huntress, the time Apollo was almost banished to Tartarus; all these were nothing compared to the pain I felt watching Mike cry. I could not take it. I stood up and looked him in the eyes. I could see my eyes reflecting back at me. There was a burning fire lighting my eyes.

"No more crying, Mike. I love you, but I have to do this and so does your dad! You will have Brooke back. Maybe we will get out, but I can't be sure. I know you must be strong Mike." He nodded and wiped the tears from his eyes. I kissed him on the forehead and told him I was going to see Landon. I was too tired to drive, so I closed my eyes and appeared at his front door. All of the rules Zeus had laid out for us while on earth were void as far as I was concerned. *I would do this my way,* I thought, sounding a little more like a determined teen than a goddess.

I rang the doorbell, and Landon's mother greeted me at the door. "Hello Bryn. Landon is in his room. Go right up." I smiled and thanked her. I tried to act normal as I walked with determination and as much fear. What if this was the last time I ever saw him? What if I never escaped and was never able to see his face again? My heart cracked a little more. I don't know about the other gods, but I was certainly feeling trapped between two worlds. I guess that's what Hades must have realized when he launched his attack on us during this vulnerable time. I wondered if this is what Zeus had wanted, for us to become weaker; to be torn like this. I wondered if Zeus underestimated how powerful this teenage experiment would be. Or more likely, the other gods had not fallen in love and were on track with Zeus. Maybe it was just me. I felt stupid, and vulnerable, and hurt, and confused. I tried to focus. I tapped his door lightly three times. Landon called to enter, and my heart pounded. Please don't let this be the last time I see him.

"Landon?" I whispered. The second he heard my voice he jerked out of bed and rushed to me, pulled me into a hug and kissed me.

"Bryn, you're back. Oh thank God!" He smiled brightly. I pulled his face down and kissed him. I knew that if it was the last time I was going to see him, and I was going to the Underworld tomorrow anyway. I needed to make the best of this moment. He stared deep into my eyes, and I guess he saw pain and torture there. "Honey, what's wrong?" he asked in his caring way. I was thrilled and amazed that he could see right through me. I didn't know a human was able to read my emotions so perfectly.

"I have to leave tomorrow. It's a family thing. I don't know when I'll be back or if I will ever be back," I uttered. My voice cracked. "And I…I can't leave you, Mike and Brooke. I'm just so heartbroken," I curled into his arms. Landon held me, and then he looked into my eyes. He looked as broken as I felt. He opened his mouth like he was going to say something, but his mouth shut closed. I knew the feeling. The feelings were too strong and the words just weren't enough. There weren't any words that would do justice to the feelings we had. Tears started to stream down my face, warm, salty tears that fell to the carpet and left small wet marks. This was the third time

I had ever cried in my life. He took my hand and led me to the couch in the back of the room and just held me while I cried. He wrapped one arm around me and stroked my hair with the other. He just let me cry, and I did. Thousands of years of being tough, years of trying so hard to never show any emotion came pouring out of me. He didn't ask me to explain; he just let me cry. After what felt like hours, he spoke.

"Do you have to leave?" His voice sounded small and worried like my next words would choose his fate for eternity. They would definitely choose mine, but I knew he would be fine without me. It would probably be safer if he forgot about me anyway.

"Yes, this is very important. Remember how I told you I was different. I'm sorry Landon. I can't really explain, and there is so much about where I am going that I don't completely understand. Please know, I wish I could stay more than anything. It's just that my family can be very, um, drastic if I don't follow their wishes. I'm so sorry." My words sounded like a pathetic excuse, and I hated that.

"When will you be back?" he asked me, determined that I would return.

"I have no idea," I told him honestly. He stared right through my eyes and said nothing. His eyes welled up with tears, and just as a single tear hit the floor, the door to his room burst open. Standing in the doorway was Apollo. My jaw dropped open in fear and embarrassment.

"Bryn, may I have a word please?" His voice was short, and I could tell something important had happened.

"Excuse me, but who are you?" Landon demanded. His voice was tainted with jealousy and fear. Apollo had entered Landon's room in his Greek god form. He was amazingly handsome. He filled the doorway with his regal presence.

"Oh I'm so sorry! I forgot to introduce myself, my name is Apollo. I am Bryn's twin brother. I'm so sorry to barge in, I just need to have a quick word with my sister, and she hasn't kept her phone with her like I asked her to. If you don't mind, this should just take a minute."

"Brother? Ok, no go ahead!" Poor Landon sounded petrified. I had just told him how difficult my family was, and then Apollo bursts into his bedroom.

"Thanks, Landon! I will be right back!" I followed Apollo into a guest bedroom and shut the door. "Wow! Very creative cover. I'm sure Landon won't suspect anything unusual when a Greek god appears in his bedroom! I am still trying to maintain my secret identity with him. What are you doing here?" I asked excitedly. Apollo laughed, and then his usually cheerful eyes turned stormy.

"Hades has taken my daughter. Like Brooke, she is trapped in the Underworld. I'm telling you Artemis, when I get my hands on that undead son of a—"

"Apollo! Hush! He could be listening. We can see what is happening. It's happened to me, Aphrodite, and now you. Hades is launching a full attack on all of us. I had a vision in my dream where all our loved ones were locked in some sick cages in the Underworld. Hades has some plan to trap all of us when we try to rescue them. Let me finish saying goodbye to Landon, and we can get the gods together to plan our strategy."

He nodded, then opened the door and composed himself enough to walk downstairs to say goodbye to Landon's parents. As soon as he reached the street, he burst into a column of fire and left a very surprised cat with a blackened tail. Before he disappeared, he yanked a tree out by its roots and kicked open a fire hydrant, leaving his mark on the street. I just sighed and walked back to Landon's room. "I'm so sorry for my brother's surprise visit. Are you OK?" I asked.

"Your brother looks a lot like you! Though there is something different about him." Well there's the fact that he was in his god form or the fact that he was so mad his eyes had actually turned into miniature suns. Either one would work. "His name is Apollo? Like the Greek god Apollo? Lord of the sun?" He asked. I wanted to add and medicine, poetry, archery, and prophesy, but I decided it was better not to. Poor Landon was stunned as he was.

"Yes, he is named after *that* Apollo," I lied in an attempt to explain. I hoped he wouldn't ask too many questions, because I didn't have any answers I could actually give him.

"The name suits him," he replied. "And, I think if you have to leave soon, we might as well take advantage of the little time we have left," he said as he pulled me into his chest. For the next few minutes we sat on that old couch and talked. I wanted desperately to tell him everything. I wanted to strategize with him, to get his advice, to beg for his help, but I held my tongue. During those moments that couch became my new favorite place. I watched every passing minute on the clock that hung on Landon's wall, knowing my time with him was drawing to an end. That's when the sadness set in. I wrapped my arms around him and just hugged and kissed him. I could not get myself to let go. I forced myself to think of Brooke and the others. I knew I had important business at hand. They were counting on me.

As we walked outside, Landon was shocked to see scorch marks, a fallen tree and broken fire hydrant in front of his house. I walked past casually, as if I didn't really notice. If he thought *that* was destruction, he had no idea what was about to come.

He drove me to Mike's house and kissed me one last time. I took in every second of it, and then I went inside. My hopes were still pinned on the fact that I might be able to get to see him again, even if it was just from a distance.

Inside the house, I could hear Mike pleading for Apollo to stay. Apollo's angry reply boomed through the house. When they heard me come in, the fighting stopped and they both looked up. Mike looked beaten, as if he had just lost a fistfight. Apollo's eyes shone brightly like fiery suns. "Hey Apollo! I love the remodeling you did on Landon's street," I said to try to break the tension in the room. He gave one of his famous smiles.

"Yeah, I have decided to put remodeling on my long list of godly talents. I'm sorry, I lost it for a second there," he said as the fiery suns diminished in his eyes and they returned to their normal, icy blue. "Artemis, we need to talk about what is going to happen tomorrow. Mike thinks we should fight Hades, but I don't think that is possible," he said as he looked to me for answers. I returned the hungry gaze and for the next few hours we cried, fought, whispered, and discussed. We decided there was no other choice but to fight for our loved ones. We planned our strategy carefully, knowing there were innocent lives on the line.

"Please don't worry about us. We will be back," I explained to Mike. "I know your dad can be harsh sometimes, but he means well. Tell Landon I'm sorry I had to leave so soon. Tell your mother thank you for all that she did for me when I was here. You need to trust that your father and I are very strong. We have been through bigger battles than this one. And we won," I told him as I kissed him on the forehead. As we walked outside, it was pouring rain. It rarely ever rained with this kind of intensity in South Texas. I assumed it was a message from Zeus to Apollo and me. I wasn't doing a great job deciphering Zeus's messages currently, so I decided to ignore them. If it was a sign, I certainly didn't know what he was trying to tell us. I grabbed Apollo's hand. We waved to Mike, closed our eyes, and when we opened them again we had arrived at the gates of the Underworld.

We stood outside the gates of the Asphodel Meadows, the interim location that is neither Heaven nor Hell. It was like Purgatory where undetermined souls wandered. If the souls tried to speak, their voices sounded like the twitter of bats. Guarding the gates was a giant three-headed dog, named Cerberus. He was there to keep any living thing out of the Underworld. The dog came down to sniff us, but I waved it off. The dog knew we were gods and went back to inspecting the spirits crossing the river Styx. We passed the large iron gates into vast, open fields. The iron gates were made of heavy rods. The rods were strong and steady, but at the top of each rod was movement. The rods themselves acted as a repellent, ready to swat off any spirit who dared try to climb it.

When we stepped into the fields, we were instantly surrounded by spirits speaking gibberish and grabbing at our clothes. They darted around us in an annoying yet fascinating way. More of them began to hover around us until we could hardly move forward.

We pushed through, shoving them away. They crowded around us. We had to keep our hands outstretched as we walked forward so we would not become overwhelmed. A girl of about sixteen years reached out to grab my hand, and Apollo stopped dead in his tracks. It was his daughter, the one he was coming to rescue. She stood there, dead, her body transparent and her eyes unseeing. Suddenly Apollo burst into a column of fire that burned hotter than the fields of punishment. From thin air appeared his chariot of fire drawn by large, white horses. He grabbed his daughter and me and threw us into his chariot. He whipped his reins, and the white stallions flew into the air, their manes of fire fluttering. We rose high over the fields, leaving the spirits confused and actively waving their arms at us.

We flew over the fields of punishment, where wicked people and those who had offended the gods during their lives were serving their time. They were tortured for the rest of eternity in these endless, desolate fields of horror. Past the fields we could see a bright shining oasis. It was Elysium, where good, kind, brave souls spent their eternity. It was a place full of large mansions, with happiness and positive energy exuding from every square inch. Finally, we flew over a large, blue lake with an island situated in the middle with white sand beaches and a dense jungle. This was the place where souls went if they chose to be reincarnated. By being admitted into Elysium three times, a soul came here, the isles of the blessed. It was breathtaking. Despite the terror I knew we were about to encounter, I was lifted by the beauty and euphoria of the scene below.

Reality returned when we flew straight through the window of Hades' castle and into the throne room, making a very grand entrance. We sent a shower of black glass over everything as we crashed into the room. Before the chariot even touched the ground Apollo jumped out erupting in to a column of fire. He gripped Hades' robes, searing off the gold lining. "Hades, you killed my daughter! We had a deal. You broke it, and now you will pay for what you did!" He whipped out his dagger and cut a deep gash down the side of Hades' face. Gold blood of the gods poured down to the marble floor. Hades cursed and pushed Apollo to the floor with a loud crash, but he instantly rose and slit Hades' arm before he even knew what had happened.

"Enough! Apollo, my nephew. Must we be so violent? It was just one daughter; you have so many more." Apollo exploded in anger. His usually beautiful face was contorted in pain and agony. In response to this, he threw Hades to the floor and pulled out his bow, but before he could shoot, Hades jumped on top of him. Hades snapped Apollo's golden bow in half. Apollo lunged and stuck his dagger in the god's calf, then rolled under his legs to escape being captured. The decorated floor flowed with golden blood. Hades was fast and grabbed Apollo's dagger from his hands and pulled him to the ground. Just as Hades was about to stab Apollo, the sun god burst into flames again, searing Hades hands.

This was getting ugly fast. I needed to help but if I did, Brooke might die. I stood and watched my brother jump on Hades' shoulders, wrapping his muscular arms around Hades' neck. Hades desperately tried to throw him off, but my brother's strength kept Hades in place. Apollo began bashing Hades' head with his clenched fists.

"Apollo, Hades! Can we please act our ages here?" A sweet liquid voice came from across the room. There stood Hera, queen of the gods. I was wondering when someone else would show up. I was hoping for almost anyone but Hera. In my list of least favorite gods, she ranked number two in a tie behind her husband and Hades. Hera had thrown her own son Hephaestus off Olympus the day he was born because she found him to be ugly. She put a curse on my mother and sent the giant serpent Python after her. She was hardly a welcomed sight to me.

Hera tried to appeal to the fighting gods, "Now, now, I know that killing Hades would give us all a little joy, Apollo, but must we be so haste? We don't want to lose our mortal or demigod friends here now, do we? Let's please stop fighting and find a civil answer to our problem."

"No Hera, you don't understand. He killed my daughter! He broke his oath and for that he must be punished." Apollo fired the words at the goddess. I could tell by the way he addressed her, he held as little respect for her as I did.

"Oh? Well, Hades I see you have created quite a problem here, haven't you?"

"Even in my own castle I can't escape your nagging. Fine. Apollo's daughter will gain Elysium. I apologize Apollo, but it was not I who killed her. She tried to slip out of the cage. She died instantly. I forgot how fragile a demigod's life is. I did not break my vow, but you both must stay for her to live." Apollo simmered so the fire only burned in his eyes and on the tips of his fingers. Soon the fire flickered out from his fingers and slowly disappeared from his eyes. In its place was the pain of losing, something Apollo did not take well. To be honest, no god really did.

Hades then handed me the key to Brooke's cage. I walked over and unlocked her. A strange sound echoed off the walls when the cage opened. It sounded like someone taking his last breath. When the door was open, she ran out and threw her arms around my neck.

"Bryn! I mean Artemis, are you sure about this? Is my life really worth more than the life of a goddess?"

"Brooke, I can not die. Not completely. We will be back, but go home for now and stay strong. I love you, Brooke." I threw my arms around her neck and kissed her forehead. Then I squeezed her and watched as she was flashed back home. The second she was gone, I stepped inside the cage. The door slammed shut, and the strange sound echoed through the room again. Soon after the door had closed, a ghost dressed in black came to collect the key that I held tightly in my hand. He stuck his gloved hand through the cage and awaited the key. I gingerly placed it in his hand, careful not to touch his hand. Apollo took his daughter's cage. The pain in his eyes tortured me as I watched him. I couldn't even imagine his pain. I knew he was blaming himself. He had not acted fast enough, and she was gone.

Throughout the rest of the day each god and goddess slowly filed in and took their mortal or demigod's place in the diamond cages. Zeus was the last to enter. He came at seven in the morning. He was ill-tempered and didn't even acknowledge that Hades was in the room. When he grabbed the key from Hades, it sent an electrical shock through Hades' body, which made Zeus smile as he made his way to his cage. He assumed the place for a young demigod. I wondered who she was. I didn't recognize her, but she seemed relieved as she was the last one to be replaced. She quickly left, and he slammed the door and threw the key across the room at Hades.

"Brothers, sisters, cousins, I welcome you to my humble home," Hades bellowed. "I'm glad all of you came and were able to set your little friends free. My deepest regrets, Apollo, for your unfortunate situation. Things happen, as they say. But, I am so grateful to each of you for attending our meeting." Apollo shook the cage in reaction.

"You have us locked up like animals, Hades," Ares screamed. "This is extortion. This is outrageous. This is not a meeting!" He ranted from his cage from the corner of the room. Everyone else mumbled their agreement.

"Plus, Hades, we all want to kill you so let's get down to business. Why are we here?" Dionysus, the god of wine, slurred from behind bars of his cage. His bottle of wine fell from his hands and shattered on the marble floor.

"No offense brother, but locking us up changes nothing. It's not like locking us up automatically gives all of our powers to you." Poseidon commented. "We came to free those we love. Now, it is time to deal with you. You have us here, so please tell us. What is it that you want, Hades?"

"I may not have all of your powers, dear brother, but I am finally in charge. You will all listen to me for a change. While I have been banished down here for eternity, you have all been free to do as you like. But, Kronos is waking. I have a chance to change my whole existence! He will give my job to some minor god, and I will be free of this hell hole forever! All I had to do was get all of you out of the way. Now father will reward me!"

The room fell silent. We all knew Hades was horrible, but stooping this low? This was out of character even for him.

"Must we remind you that when you were born, Kronos ate you to keep you from overthrowing him?" Zeus spoke for the first time.

"This is insane, Hades! You are going to give everything back to the Titans? They will kill all the humans and destroy Earth as we know it! They are using you. They won't honor their promises. They will banish you and the rest of us to Tartarus when they are done with you!" Demeter screamed in protest. Demeter was the goddess of the harvest. As she spoke, wheat erupted from the marble floors and began to wrap around Hades' ankles. He ripped his ankles away, but it grew out of the marble and followed him. It was as if the wheat was trying to consume him.

"Enough from all of you! I will do what I will do. You will not rule over me anymore," Hades declared as he stormed out of the room. We all stood in silence staring at Demeter's magical wheat growing from the marble floor. I tried to get Apollo's attention, but he had shut himself off from everyone. He cradled his head in his hands and stared at the floor.

"What? Are we just going to let Kronos and the Titans win? If another war of the gods and Titans happens Gaea *will* wake up! If that happens, we won't have to worry about stupid Hades, because she will take us all down. If Kronos is rising, other Titans will return. It would be complete chaos if everyone returns." I shouted. "Gaea might be mother earth, but she is going to be one crazy mother if she wakes after thousands of years to find us in battle. A war would be the doom of us all. We have to make sure Gaea stays in the ground where she belongs," I pleaded.

"Artemis is right. We must stop Hades. We need to show him why he should be on our side," Hephaestus added.

"How are we going to do that? We haven't exactly wanted him with us. We can't ask him to please be on our side now because it suits us. As a tactical strategy, it's weak and ineffective to suddenly declare our desire for our long lost brother whom we have ignored for thousands of years. He will never accept that from us, and quite frankly I don't blame him. It makes sense that he has associated with the Titans while we have all been happily living our lives on Olympus. He was banished from his family, to a life of the caretaker of the Underworld. He has grown accustomed to death and destruction. He deals with it every day. I would have gone insane if I was him," Athena said more to herself than anyone else. Being the goddess of wisdom and strategy she listened, watched, and planned. I was hoping she would share a plan with the rest of us, but after she spoke she sat thinking deeply.

Athena was my favorite of my family after Apollo. I continued to watch her. Suddenly, she looked as if a light went on inside that amazing mind of hers. She turned to face the others and spoke. "Yes, we need to find a way to convince Hades that he does not have a better life ahead of him with the Titans. Right now, he would rather be ruled by Kronos than stay here in the Underworld. We have to offer Hades a better plan," Athena told us.

"So what do you suggest, Athena, oh mighty goddess of wisdom? Why do we always have to listen to you?" Ares taunted. "I'm ready to get out of this dammed cage and go take Hades right now!"

"Oh, Ares. You are always so ready for a fight, you sometimes forget to think first," Athena replied.

"Stop bickering!" Hera screamed. She hated fighting. "Ares, let Athena finish. We need you as the god of war *outside* of this room, not *inside* it! Until then, please try to listen so we can all be ready for the battle when it comes. Athena, go on."

"Right now our best strategy is to wait and watch. To act rashly would lead to our demise. We need to methodically plan our escape. We can't do anything locked in these cages, so escape must be our first plan. We need everyone working together in ways we have never done before." The room fell silent. The goddess of strategy was telling us she wanted us to come up with a plan and a strategy. We were in a lot of trouble.

We sat in silence waiting for a plan to emerge. Our thoughts were interrupted as Hades burst through the large black and gold double doors. In tow was a beautiful lady in a dress made entirely of flowers. Her long amber hair was flowing down to her lower back. Persephone. She was the goddess of flowers, daughter of Demeter, a minor goddess, and the bride of Hades. As a young girl, she was captured by Hades while she was picking flowers and was held hostage. Though she was rescued, it was not soon enough. She had eaten six seeds from a pomegranate grown in the Underworld. The rule was, if you ate anything that had grown in the Underworld, you had to stay in the Underworld. The six seeds she had eaten sentenced her to live in the Underworld for six months of every year. She served her time in the Underworld during the winter. I assume so she could still enjoy the flowers on earth during the spring and summer. She was beautiful, but she looked miserable as she walked alongside Hades. She looked up from her sulking to see all of her family locked up in cages. She screamed.

"In the name of all things Olympus! What have you done?" Her voice was shaking and her face was red with anger. "Mom!" She ran to Demeter's cage and put her hand through the bars and stroked her mother's hair. "You demon! You are a horrible monster! What have you done, Hades? How is this going to help anything? You promised me. You promised you would try harder. Then you go and do this. They already don't like you!"

"Darling, don't get yourself so upset. This is the beginning of our new life! Kronos will reward us. We will be treated better than we have ever been treated before. You will be released with me, and we can live together on earth."

"Let them go!" she spat back at him.

"I'm sorry, honey. I can't do that. Now please go to your garden, calm down and come back when you have a rational head on your shoulders." She silently closed her eyes and pointed below Hades feet. Suddenly, twenty-foot roses grew rapidly from the ground and wrapped their thorns around the god. The roses tied him up in a nest of thorns, lifting him slightly off the floor.

"There, I played in my garden. And, you're right; I feel a lot better. I still hate you, and you're not coming down from there until you agree to let them go. But I do feel better." Hades sighed as though this happened every day. He closed his eyes and the flowers slowly started to shrivel and die. Persephone stomped her foot and stormed out of the room leaving behind a trail of poisonous flowers that spelled out "Hades is evil". All the gods laughed at the display. Hades finally got the roses to wilt, and he walked down and approached his caged family members. He smiled a devilish smile.

"Well my dear family, it seems I have some matters to attend to with the Titans. But while I'm gone I have left some entertainment for you. I have hooked up a small computer screen inside of your cages and some headphones. I thought you would want to watch what is happening to the hero or mortal that you came here to save. You will be able to see how they are enjoying the life you gave back to them. Let's see if you made the right choice. Honestly, the time you have spent with humans has made you soft. Enjoy." He sneered and then with a puff of black smoke was gone. I reached for the headphones and turned on the small monitor. Immediately Brooke's face flashed across the screen. Her eyes were filled with worry and confusion. She was back at her house, and I could tell she was trying to decide if she had been dreaming the whole horrible event or if it had actually happened. She ran inside her house and threw her arms around her parents.

"Hi dear, how was Bryn?" At first she looked confused, but thankfully Brooke was accustomed to telling her parents what they wanted to hear. She caught on quickly.

"Oh, she was great! Would you mind if I stayed a few more days? Bryn really needs me right now. Her parents are being really difficult. They seem to be easier on her when I'm around. That's why I'm so thankful to have you two." She hugged them both, and that did the trick. They looked lovingly at their sweet daughter and agreed to her request. I could only imagine what she was planning.

She kissed them, ran upstairs, and packed a small bag and ran outside. She was driving to Mike's house like a mad woman. Her knuckles were turning white, and I was scared she was going to hit something or someone. She almost hit three cars, and she actually ran two red lights. When she finally got to Mike's house she hopped out of her car and dashed inside without knocking. At first, Mike looked a little shocked but then relived and finally worried. He ran to her and threw his arms around her and picked her up in a huge embrace. He kissed her lightly and then set her back down on the ground.

"Brooke! Oh thank my father Apollo you're ok!" he smiled. Thank Apollo? *Thank Apollo?* Who did he think saved her? I swear, demigods sometimes.

"Mike, Bryn—I mean Artemis is in big trouble. Hades said he was setting the Titans free and the gods would forever rot in Tartarus. They need our help. We need to save them!" She was pacing around the room trying to find the words to describe how grave the situation was. He looked as white as a sheet, and he grabbed his kitchen counter to support himself.

"Did you say Hades was releasing the T-T-Titans?" His voice stuttered when he got to the word Titan. Brooke nodded, and Mike's face was ashen. "That's not good; that's very bad."

"Why, who are the Titans?" Brooke asked innocently.

"They were the rulers at the beginning of mankind, when everyone lived in fear and darkness. They were the parents of the gods. Zeus overthrew the leader, Kronos, who was technically his own father. The rest of the gods, the ones who were there at the time of the Titans, helped overthrow the rest of the Titan rulers. Then man was created, and well, you know the rest. The Titans are evil and would do anything to overthrow Olympus. Why Hades would help them rise is unknown to me. He helped overthrow them in the first place. He must want to rise out of the Underworld so badly he will risk everything. The way he is going about it is extremely dangerous. If he succeeds, we can kiss all of mankind goodbye."

"So, we are going to go rescue them right?" Brooke pleaded.

"I'm not sure. It's going to be very dangerous. Messing with a god like Hades, when he is trying to raise the very powerful Titans, is not encouraged by anyone. Someone's going to get hurt. I mean really hurt."

As I was listening to them talk I wanted to jump through the screen or scream out to them. They could not come help us. They would get themselves killed!

"Mike, we are going! We don't have a choice," Brooke cried.

"Fine, but we're going to need someone's help first."

# Chapter Ten

Mike grabbed Brooke's hand and pulled her out the door into the drizzling rain. Even the weather knew something bad was about to happen. I watched Mike drive chaotically through the streets. Brooke clutched the back of her seat so tightly I swore she would never be able to get her fingernails out of the leather. Mike swerved down Landon's street and came to a screeching halt in front of his house. The color slowly started to return to Brooke's face. "What are we doing here?" Brooke asked in a shaky voice, still dazed from Mike's driving.

"Landon needs to help us get back the gods. He is a black belt in Tae Kwon Do, so his fighting skills will be helpful, but that's not the real reason we are here. You see, Hades is hoping the gods won't try to escape because they would be too afraid he would kill all of the mortals they care about. That would cause some serious suspicion. The new kid comes, then disappears, and suddenly all the friends they made are dead. The mortal world would turn into a state of panic. If Landon comes with us, Hades will have no one to kill back home and Artemis can protect us while we are with her. With our help, she will gain control back over Hades. If we leave Landon at home and Artemis escapes, he will threaten to kill Landon. Our only option is to take him with us. She will stay there to try to keep him alive if we come without him." Mike explained.

I was impressed. I listened to Mike and realized he had a very clear understanding of the gods. Brooke nodded as if she understood, and they made their way up the steps to Landon's house. Brooke halfheartedly knocked on the door, and Landon peeked his head out. Black circles etched under his eyes like he had gotten no sleep last night. He gestured for them to come inside. "Landon we need to talk to you. It's about Bryn. Is there somewhere we can talk privately?" Mike asked while looking around the room for anyone who might be hiding.

"My parents are at work; it's just me. I decided not to go to school today. We can talk here." Landon gestured to the couch. Even in sadness his eyes still melted my soul. My heart broke in two. Even with no sleep his hair looked perfect and his rosy red lips stood out on his tan face. He sat on the couch, across from the one Brooke and Mike had taken. "So she left?" Landon's voice cracked when he asked. The pain on his face suddenly became evident.

"Landon, she did not leave for the reason you think. We need to tell you, but you have to be open-minded. Everything I'm about to tell you is true, and Bryn is in trouble, real trouble. We have to save her or she is going to die. Your world is about to fall apart; everything you thought you knew is going to be undone. Brace yourself." This seemed to get Landon's full attention, and he promised to listen. "You know the stories of the Greek gods?" Landon nodded, "Well they are not stories. Every one of them is completely true. The Greek gods are all real, and more importantly, they still exist today. I know this because I'm the son of Apollo. I'm a demigod." Landon's eyes bulged and his jaw dropped.

"Is Bryn a demigod?" Landon asked harshly.

"No, this is where it gets more mind-bending for you. Bryn is a goddess." Mike took a deep breath and continued. "She is Artemis, goddess of the moon and hunt. Hades tried to capture Brooke, but she gave herself in Brooke's place. Now Hades has Artemis and ten other gods captured in the Underworld. He is going to try to release the Titans, destroy the other gods, and destroy the world as we know it. We have to go to the Underworld and save the gods before Hades can raise the Titans. But we can't do it without you." Then Mike went on to explain what he had told Brooke in the car about why they needed him. Landon nodded in agreement.

"It actually explains a lot about her. So many things make sense about her now. Her slip-up in calling herself Artemis. The waiter calling her Artemis, and her brother Apollo. I believe you, but what is your plan to defeat Hades in the Underworld?"

"Well, let's hope we are not the only people coming to save the gods. There should be other demigods and mortals coming to do exactly what we are doing. That's what we are hoping for." Mike sounded more like he was trying to convince himself than Landon.

"Wait! You said your dad is Apollo? That means…"

"Yes, Artemis is my aunt." At that point Landon looked uncomfortable. His reaction was strange. I couldn't quite put my finger on what he must have been thinking. He shifted awkwardly in his chair.

"If you think that's bad, it also means your girlfriend is like millions of years old!" Mike laughed. Landon took a deep breath as he tried to take in everything he had just learned. Then he looked at Brooke who had been strangely quiet during the whole conversation.

"Brooke, are you a demigod too?" Landon asked.

"No, I'm a mortal too, but I can see through the veil that hides the monsters and gods from most humans. There are a few other humans like me who where born without the veil. Artemis also told me that once a mortal with the veil discovers the truth, the veil will start to lift. But, yes I'm like you, no godly parent, no special powers, and I had never known about any of this god stuff before Bryn came here." Brooke explained. Landon didn't seem to be listening to a word Brooke was saying. His look was calculating and brooding.

"Wait, why did Artemis come here? I mean why would a goddess come to a random high school in

Texas? Why here? Why is she Bryn?" His voice seemed stronger, angrier.

"Well, Zeus decided it would be a great way for the gods to get in touch with this generation of people. He forced all of the major gods to choose a high school to enroll in." Mike made the plan sound like a sweet innocent idea that Zeus thought would really help us, not a plan that went very, very wrong. Landon nodded like he understood. "So will you help us?"

"Of course. So, if Bryn is actually Artemis, that is the reason she kept running away from me. Artemis swore off men. She wasn't really rejecting me; she was rejecting men in general." As Landon spoke, I was surprised how much he actually knew about me, Artemis. Most teenage boys I had met weren't as well read as Landon was in Greek mythology. It made me happy and a little uncomfortable at the same time. Although I had sworn off men, I was still in control of my decisions. It wasn't an ancient curse that had me not be with Landon; it was my decision to continue my vow.

I turned my head away from the screen and back to what was happening in Hades' courtroom. A couple of the gods were watching the screens intently. Ares was violently stabbing his screen with a spear, but every time he did the TV would fix itself. Then Ares would stab it again. As I looked around the room, I saw that the screen served as a distraction for most all of us. We weren't spending our time planning; we were too busy focusing on our loved ones on the screens. Dionysus, however, sat in the corner of his cage pounding wine and mumbling to himself about zebras, I think. I sat there terrified. My mortal friends were all about to risk their lives for me, and I was stuck in a diamond cage, from which none of us could escape.

Suddenly, Hades stormed into the room, and it fell silent, except for Dionysus who was still mumbling in the corner. He started throwing his wine bottles at Hermes' cage, singing and mumbling. Hades bowed graciously toward us in mock respect. "Dear family, I have fabulous news! The Titans, as it turns out, have actually been working on rising up for quite some time. It seems that a couple of them have actually freed themselves already. I understand Prometheus is out and has quite a bone to pick with you, Zeus." Hades sneered.

Prometheus was a Titan who was not killed during the first war because he was not a threat to the gods and did not want to overthrow them. Prometheus gave man fire, even though Zeus had strictly told him not to. In return for his disobedience, Zeus strapped him to the side of a mountain and had vultures rip him apart every day. The birds tore at his flesh and ate it. Every night he would heal and return to normal, and the torture would begin again. It made sense that Prometheus would want to destroy Zeus. The more I heard about Hades' plan, the deeper my stomach sank. "Now I have an offer for each of you. If any of you wish to join me, you will be spared from the revenge of the Titans. You can join the Titan army and be part of the new era. You will remain a god or goddess and will be spared the impending wrath. Join me, and you will have more power than you have ever had before." We all sat there listening and staring at Hades as he spoke. Even the gods who had been watching their screens looked up to glare at Hades in disgust.

"Hades, and I mean total offense when I say this, are you stupid? Do you really think any of us would join you? You locked us in cages and almost killed our mortal friends and children. You are trying to destroy everything we have created. Why would we help you?" Poseidon spat back at Hades. Hades nodded sadly.

"Well brother, I'm sorry that you feel this way, but I guess we will have to give the ocean back to Oceanus." Hades smiled wickedly, and Poseidon let a loud growl.

"Oceanus! That old Titan has not seen the ocean let alone ruled it in millions of years! He has no idea how it has changed. You're going to give it back to him?" Zeus bellowed. Little bolts of electricity started to form around him. He was so mad; he was creating a lightning storm around him. "So I guess that means Kronos is taking back over everything else? He is going to rule a world he has been absent from for so many years? You're insane, Hades. Do you really think Kronos will spare you? He will banish you to Tartarus as soon as he gains full power. He is just using you as a pawn! Why can't you see that?" For the first time, in a very long time, Zeus was making sense to me.

"Zeus, my dear brother, for the king of the gods you don't seem to understand a lot, do you? That is what you would do if you were rising back to power. We all know you would have pawns, and then you would destroy them. But this time we are not talking about you. Yes, I know I fought against them in the first Titan war, but I'm going to help raise them again. That will wipe my slate clean. Now don't be stupid and join me! Continue to rule! You don't have to give up all your power." Hades offered.

"Hades, you are crazy. The Titans are never going to work with you, and Zeus will never be forgiven. I mean, Kronos ate his own children. Do you think he's going to work with any of us?" Poseidon said, almost to himself. He was right of course. When Rhea, the Titan, gave birth to the children she had with Kronos, he swallowed the children because of a prediction from the oracle, that fortold his undoing by one of his children. Rhea hid Zeus from Kronos and as he grew she began to plot with him on how to overthrow his father. Zeus succeeded in this task, and chopped Kronos to pieces before tossing him into Tartarus. There was no way Kronos would ever forgive Zeus for that act of betrayal.

"Poseidon, don't try to reason with him. It's not worth it. Hades, even if Kronos would forgive me I would never join him. I will do everything in my power to keep Kronos from gaining power," Zeus bellowed.

"Very well then, if none of you will join me, I hope you enjoy your cages. Oh, this is great. While you all are stuck in the Underworld, I will be up on Olympus planning my new era. Oh how the tables have turned. Enjoy the dead!"

"Wait, Hades!" Dionysus called. Everyone gasped. Would he really join them? Hades turned around an evil glint in his eyes.

"Yes?" he asked with a smug tone.

"You shouldn't go outside! You have been down in darkness for so long you might melt, you evil demon."

He mumbled in a drunken slur from the floor of his cage. Everyone was quiet as Hades stormed out of the room. The second he was gone, the room erupted into loud arguments. Even in the face of the destruction of the world, we could not work together.

"If I could get out of this cage, I would strangle that good for nothing," Ares rattled off a list of ancient Greek curses.

"Now Ares, my dear son, cursing out Hades will get us nowhere. We need a plan, and we need one fast. Hades will try to raise Kronos, if he hasn't already. I have no wish to see my father again." Hera cooed. I watched and listened with fascination knowing that Hera and Zeus are brother and sister, and they are married. Their relationship had always confirmed my decision to swear off men. Relationships for the gods are usually unusual and complicated. Being a maiden forever was a better option.

"I don't know how many of you have been watching your screens, but my mortal friends and one of Apollo's sons have decided to come and try to free us. If I could somehow tell them to find my huntresses, we might actually have a shot at escaping." I spoke up for the first time in a while. Everyone nodded and some of them said they had demigods coming to help, too.

"Go to sleep Artemis, and try to reach someone," Athena commanded, "Remember to get there in your dreams. We should all try it. Our imprisonment can't stop us from reaching our loved ones through our dreams. We should still be able to reach someone who can help." I couldn't imagine falling to sleep at this moment, but I knew how to transform myself into a sleep state. I had done it every time I needed something I could not get my hands on immediately. I could do this.

I nodded and lay down on the small bed in the corner of the cage. It had a silver, crescent moon on the blankets and pillows. Hades must have needed a reminder which mortal belonged to which god or goddess. As soon as my head hit the pillow I drifted off to sleep. My first dream was of a deep, dark pit, and rising was a single golden light. A deep booming laugh echoed off the rocks. It sent goose bumps up my arms.

"Hello Artemis. Haven't you grown up into a great goddess? Well my dear granddaughter, I know why your dreams sent you here first. You do too don't you? You know that joining the Titans might be your best option." I tried to yell but my voice would not work. "Oh save it, you can't talk in this dream. This is my monologue. Now listen. You have broken your oath to never love a man. You put your huntresses in a vulnerable position by leaving them and breaking your oath. But you can join us. They won't have the same allegiance to you now that you have abandoned them. You really have no reason to return to Olympus without us. We will even save the mortal boy you love! He can be immortal and live with you forever. Just think about it will you? If you decide to join us, just let Hades know." Then that same booming laugh echoed off the walls and drilled its way into my heart. My head started to spin and the gold light seemed to brighten and grow a little closer to the top. Kronos was rising from Tartarus.

Suddenly the dream shifted, and I was sitting in the back of Mike's old Mustang. It was quiet as Mike drove in the rain. Mike and Brooke held hands in the front seat and Landon sat in the back looking depressed. I hoped my voice would work in this dream. "Hey guys," I uttered. Despite feeling desperate, my voice sounded strong. Mike slammed on the brakes and looked around in confusion.

"Bryn! Where are you?" Landon asked excitedly.

"I'm not really with you. I'm visiting you from a dream. I'm not sure how long I have, so I will try to make this quick. We cannot escape without your help. The Titans are rising quickly, and we need to get out of here. You need to go to Olympus and find my huntresses. They will help you and find Hestia, the goddess of hearth and home. She is probably the nicest of the gods and you are going to need all the help you can get. Get help from any demigods you find on the way, but hear my warning. Get the help from no other god but Hestia. Most of the minor gods are jealous of us and are on the side of the Titans. They will trick you. Stay away from them. They cannot be trusted. I love you all, but my time here is up. The gods will be with you." Then my voice faded, and I could no longer speak. I could only observe.

"Well, I guess we're taking a road trip to Olympus." Mike laughed trying to lighten the mood. "The car will be too slow. We need a faster way to get to D.C. It's only about three hours from here by plane. We will need to leave now." They all nodded in agreement. I wondered what Landon had told his parents before he left. Oh hey mom, Bryn is actually the Greek goddess Artemis and Hades has locked her up while he tries to release the Titans. So I'm going to be gone for a while trying to save her, bye.

As they drove through the rain to the airport, my vision started to blur. I slowly started to wake up. My time back with my friends was over. My eyes refocused on the dimly lit caverns of the Underworld. I sat up and reluctantly pulled myself out of bed.

"Any luck? Did you get in touch with anyone?" Apollo started questioning me the second my toes touched the floor.

"Yeah, sleeping beauty, this better be good. While you were sleeping we were planning over here! All those years of hunting prepared you to sleep? Did you sleep in while your huntresses did all the work?" Ares taunted.

"Ares! Dear Olympus, do you ever shut up? This may come as a surprise but not everyone cares about what you have to say!" Hermes chided. Apollo, who had been unusually quiet since the recent death of his daughter, laughed aloud.

"Yes, I got in touch with Apollo's son Mike and two mortals who are on their way to Olympus to find my huntresses and Hestia." I spoke loud and strong like Ares had never even spoken.

"You told them to find Hestia?" Aphrodite asked sounding sincerely confused. "Why? What can she do?" her voice dripped with arrogance.

"I imagine she can do a lot more than you can while sitting in a cage admiring your reflection in a mirror. At least I'm trying to get help. Your vanity can not serve you right now Aphrodite. We are going to need more than beauty to get us out of this mess, so I suggest you put down your mirror and use whatever brain you have in that head!" My words were unusually harsh, but I was scared. I was sending my three favorite people on a nearly impossible mission to help save us.

"Artemis, don't let my beauty intimidate you. Just because you broke your oath and fell in teenage love, doesn't mean you have to lash out at me. Landon isn't it? I thought you had sworn off men? Cheating on your oath? You always act like you can do no wrong Artemis. Well, you really did it this time!"

Great Greek gods. How in the world did she know about Landon? She even knew his name. "Have we been spying?" I hissed, "How do you know about him? Is your life so boring that you have to peer in on mine?" The other gods mumbled to each other as our fight got more heated.

"Why Artemis dear, you're in love, and I am love itself. I know all the love that ever starts, when it ends, first kisses, and even first dates. It is what I do." She said in a very singsong voice.

"So it's true?" Hephaestus asked sounding very shocked. I nodded.

"Yes, I did break my oath. I fell in love with a mortal. Now please stop acting so shocked; you all have thousands of demigod children out there." I sighed, they might as well know. Ares' face went bright with excitement.

"That's all very exciting news, Artemis. Congrats!" Ares mocked. But, right now we have more important things to worry about than your first crush. First; why can't we escape these cages?"

"You don't know?" Hephaestus asked as if he was shocked that none of us already knew. "They are crafted out of the two things Hades controls, death and precious stones. He made the cages out of diamonds and then enveloped them in death. The only way you can escape the cage is to die. You can walk through the bars, but you're dead once you reach the other side. As gods we can't actually die, so we can't walk through the barrier. Watch." He pushed his hand up against the space between two bars. His hand was suddenly wrinkled and his arm looked withered, like a very old man. Then he pulled his hand away, and it returned to normal. Even Athena looked shocked. How could Hades make a cage out of death? How would he even know something like that was possible? I touched my finger to the cage. I felt a sudden hollow chill as my finger transformed into a grey, lifeless skin I didn't recognize. I truly felt like I was on death's door. I quickly pulled my finger away from the cage. I stumbled into my bed with a loud thud. This was all worse than I imagined it would be. I was confused and scared for the first time. I turned my head toward the small screen by my bed, and my heart dropped to the pits of Tartarus. It just got worse.

# CHAPTER ELEVEN

My friends stood in the fresh morning air of Washington D.C. Morning dew shone on the trees and grass. The sun danced beautifully between the leaves in the trees, and the wind tossed their hair gently. It would have been the most beautiful image I had seen in a long time if it were not for the giant that loomed over them. He was about nine feet tall, with dark, greasy hair. His face was covered with acne and the skin around his eyes was marked with red scars. He was disgusting to look at, and I literally gagged seeing him on the monitor. His name was Pityocamptes, an old monster who no one had seen since the days of an ancient demigod, Theseus. Pityocamptes was infamous for his unique brand of torture. One story of his torture included him tying a person to two trees he had pulled together. Once he let the trees go, the poor person was ripped in half. I also heard he asked a victim to help him hold down the tree and then let it go, sending his helper flying to his death. He killed those who helped him, and he killed those who wouldn't help him.

Seeing him there was not a good sign, and Mike recognized the giant as soon as he saw him. Mike's face went pale, and he pulled Brooke into his arms in a protective circle. He whispered for her to stay back, and then he stepped in front of her trying to keep her as far away from the brute as possible. Pityocamptes was smart. He turned around and spotted them and let out a little laugh. "*Ha ha ha* young heroes! Me like! They make good splat on ground. Why don't you come hold my tree? It fun, real fun. You try. Come hold my tree. Or I smash you. *Ha ha*!" The giant laughed and pulled Mike over to the tree, not even noticing Brooke. Many monsters didn't bother with mortals. Then he paused, looking over at Landon, a strange look passed over his large face. He seemed to be trying to remember something, but it quickly slipped away and he returned his attention to Mike.

"This is a very fine tree." Mike stalled, "I mean, wow, look at the bark. It's just amazing! I must ask you, how do you have such great taste in trees?" The giant blushed and patted the tree a little too hard because bark flew in every direction.

"Oh, young hero is nice. I pick pretty tree. I have good taste 'cause I smart. I just know when I see good tree. Now you hold tree." The giant commanded. Mike tried to stall for more time.

"But this tree is just too large for me. I will have to have my friends over there help me." He motioned behind him toward where Brooke and Landon were standing. Landon had a hazy look in his eyes, like he actually knew what was happening. Many mortals start to see the truth once they know about the gods, but it can take time for them to readjust. Landon seemed to recognize Pityocamptes as a giant monster immediately. A look of suspicion passed over the giant's face, but he nodded and pointed a giant, dirty finger toward the tree. Mike took Brooke's hand and motioned Landon toward the tree. They walked toward it, looking frightened. The giant bent the tree down to the point where it almost snapped. Brooke and Landon followed Mike's lead and placed their hands on the top of the straining tree. The giant chuckled, and he pretended to fuss with one of the branches.

"Ok, the giant's name is Pityocamptes and in a couple seconds he is going to let go of this tree hoping we will fly with it, and he will get a tasty demigod and mortal lunch. Theseus defeated him by holding the tree down. Do you think we can hold it"? Mikes words stumbled out of his mouth and even he seemed hesitant of his plan. But it was how Pityocamptes had been defeated before so it seemed like the only available option. The others nodded slowly, unsure of the plan. Then, as if on cue, the giant let go of the tree. The tree held it's position; it did not move. The three were actually doing it! Pride overwhelmed me. They might actually be able do this.

"Not again! I break tree? No, they holding tree? No. Not again," Pityocamptes grumbled as he bent over the tree.

"Let go now!" Mike yelled, and the tree flung with a giant thump into the giant's head. He was out cold in a number of seconds. Thankfully, the three did not wait long enough to see what happened to his body. They sprinted down the street toward the Washington Monument. They ran with all their might to make their way toward Pennsylvania Avenue.

When they got near the White House, they realized they had a big problem. How were they going to get in? Then they saw a large booth with a huge red, white, and blue banner hanging above it that read *White House Tour*. They would have to sneak in with the next group, which was slowly assembling and calling roll. "The Sterns?" a large bald man called out, slowly checking names off on his American flag clip board. He was clad in the country's colors. He looked like a walking tourist shop. On his garish shirt was a "Hello my name is—" sticker with the name BOB written in a messy scrawl. "Well it looks like we will have to start the tour without the Sterns party of two and Jackson party of two. Last call for Sterns and Jackson?" Landon's face lit up with a beautiful smile that made my heart ache.

"No, we are here! Don't start without us! I'm Jackson, actually I'm just a party of one today, and this lovely couple is the Sterns." Landon smiled at Bob.

"Umm..." The man scratched his bald head, "Well being tardy to see the White House. Hmm, not very patriotic, but I'll let it slide," he joked. "Hop on board you rabble- rousers, and let's go see the heart of this fine nation!" They walked through the gates and onto the green grass. Two large hellhounds sat in the perfectly cut lawn. They sun bathed and rolled around like two happy puppies. Mike stopped dead in his tracks. He stuck out a hand to stop Brooke. Landon seemed to be staring at the White House in amazement.

"Hellhounds," Mike mumbled. He took off his backpack and pulled out a small covered dagger. As he drew the dagger from its holder it grew into a full-length sword. He whipped it around toward the hellhounds but they just lazily looked at him and blinked. Then they yawned and went back to rolling in the grass.

"Hey! Drop that weapon! Darn demigods always coming around here acting as if everything from our world is going to bite their stupid little heads off." A short man with shaggy blonde hair darted toward them. He was wearing dirty jeans and an old baseball cap barely hiding little horns. He ran with an awkward gait, and I could see his legs were actually hooves. He stumbled toward Mike, his little face was red, and he was clearly out of breath from the short jog across the lawn. "The name's Tanner. I'm a Satyr as you can probably tell. The fact that I'm half man half goat makes me tougher, mind you. And I run the portal to Olympus in America. The hellhounds won't hurt you. So, you can put that sword away. Do you know what kind of trouble you can get in to trying to sneak a weapon into the White House? Are you crazy? You are obviously heading to the portal, right? It's on the sixth floor, but don't be dragging out another weapon on your way. They'll shoot you in here for that." He said, without seeming to take a breath. "Now off with you!" He focused on Mike and Landon with his instruction, and barely seemed to notice Brooke, who was in awe of the little man. He shooed them away, and they ran to go catch up with the rest of the tour.

During the first part of the tour Bob spoke with a passion that made me want to hoist an American flag. They all listened and followed the tour from the ground floor all the way up to the third floor. When they got there, they excused themselves to use the restroom. Brooke, Mike and Landon walked aimlessly across the top floor until they reached a room marked with the Greek symbol Omega.

Ω

"Do you think this is the room?" Mike asked.

"No, I think it's the other room in the White House marked with a letter from the Greek alphabet," Landon snapped. Mike shot him a dirty look and then turned back to the door. But before he could grab the handle, Brooke grabbed his hand.

"I don't think it's a good idea to just barge into Olympus," Brooke proclaimed. She knocked three times on the door and it pulled open. In the doorway stood a large, burly man. His name was Cantrus, and he was the guardian of Olympus. His muscles rippled through his shirt. He was large enough to eat Brooke, but thankfully he didn't. She looked up and smiled at him.

"What's your business?" His voice was scratchy like he had sand paper caught in his throat.

"Hello! We are here because we are good friends of Artemis, and we know that Hades has captured the gods. We must speak to the huntresses and Hestia. We need to free the gods." I chuckled as I listened to Brooke explain their business. She was so earnest. Anyone outside Olympus would have thought she was insane, but Cantrus understood. He looked down at her and pulled the door open as he nodded at them.

They walked through a dimly lit hallway which led to a small set of stairs. As they climbed the stairs, I watched their reactions as they gazed at the giant golden door at the top. I was sure none of them had been through this portal before. It glowed faintly in the dimly lit room. Engraved on the door were scenes of the gods and goddesses, pictorial descriptions of us defeating the Titans. Zeus throwing lightning bolts, Poseidon killing monsters with his Trident, Ares in the heat of battle, and then there was me. I stood tall in the picture with my bow drawn and a deer before me, my hair was flowing behind me. I thought I looked graceful. Landon touched my picture and smiled. "Artemis," he said weakly. I watched from afar as Landon smiled at my likeness. "She looks beautiful," he boasted. He had never actually seen me as Artemis, so it came as something of a shock that he knew me immediately.

"She's quite a beauty. She isn't really my girlfriend or anything but I guess with that 'No Man' policy, she probably can't be." Sadness filled his voice. I would make sure if I ever made it back to him, I would explain how I felt. I longed for him to know how wonderful it felt for him to call me beautiful. I would try to explain. I just hoped I would have the chance.

Cantrus opened the large, gleaming door to a place far more beautiful. "Welcome to Olympus!" He smiled. He closed the door behind them. All three of their jaws dropped at once. They stood in awe of the most beautiful city in history. The portal had taken them to the home of ancient Greece, Olympus. Majestic white marble buildings stood on rolling green hills. Each building had a large golden dome on top of it that gleamed in the sunlight. Trees lined the sidewalks and a large lake sat in the middle lined with small gazebos, trees, and flowers. A light breeze made the flower petals dance across the grass. It was a utopia.

The centerpiece of the scene was a large domed building that was larger than the others. It had gleaming brass doors and statues of all the major gods and goddess adorning the building. I longed to be there with them as they walked past all the statues toward the giant brass doors of the throne hall. The beautiful doors were etched with engravings of the realms we ruled. There were scenes of the moon and the sun which shone on opposite sides of the door, fires blazing, vast oceans, a thunderstorm, the grim Underworld, mortals at war, and beautiful flowers blooming. Hephaestus had created this magnificent masterpiece, and it blended together majestically, just like a raging river.

As they entered, the beauty overwhelmed them. It was the most beautiful place on all of Olympus. The beauty was shocking. The tall domed ceiling arched hundreds of feet high, vines snaked up the large marble walls, blooming flowers no mortal man could grow. The floor was a giant map of the stars, and each star was represented by a large diamond encased in the tiles of the floor. The showpiece of the room was the thrones, and they literally took your breath away. They were each twenty feet tall and hand-sculpted. Each throne represented each god and every one flowed with the energy of that god. Zeus's throne was a large gold chair that crackled with electricity. Strapped to the arms of the chair were his lighting bolts. Although the electric bolts shone beautifully, they were highly deadly to the touch. Hera's was a marble base, but the back of the chair was made of giant metal peacock feathers. The others were all just as glorious, each one solely created for the god it represented. Mine was made out of silver; the arms were made to look like giant bows and at the top stood a giant crescent moon. It shone like the real moon. In the dark room it was the second brightest, next to Apollo's chair of the sun.

Though I had spent so much time in this room, I had never really noticed how beautiful it was. Seeing my friends gaze in awe really made me see it with new eyes, as if I was experiencing it for the first time, too. My favorite part of the room was the fireplace. Like in most Greek homes, this room with the fireplace was located in the center of the building. It was the unofficial throne of Hestia, a sign that even though she was no longer a major goddess, we still loved her. And we truly did. Despite any of our differences, everyone loved Hestia. She never argued with anyone about anything. While the rest of us would argue over everything, she simply wanted everyone to be happy. Hestia never married, but she would have made an amazing mother. I guess she considered us her children. We sure acted like it sometimes.

"This place is unbelievable. But, what exactly are we supposed to do now?" Landon asked walking around the fireplace searching the room like a hint might be hiding somewhere.

"We are looking for the goddess Hestia, the goddess of the hearth and home. I assume that the fireplace is where we will find her as it is the hearth of this home. Maybe if we make a sacrifice into the fire and call to her, she will come," Mike guessed, but his face was a dead give away of his cluelessness. Brooke smiled and ran out of the room and into the small garden outside. She grabbed the fruits growing off the blossoming trees, and then she quickly ran back inside, threw her offerings into the fire, and then closed her eyes and prayed. In seconds, a warm glow filled the room, and Hestia appeared. Her long, brown hair flowed down to her waist; her eyes glowed with a warm pride, and her mouth filled with her beautiful smile. Her presence calmed the room as happiness exuded from her presence.

"Hello beautiful children! How may I be of service?" She bowed at them slowly. "I hear that my dear family is in trouble because of Hades. I asked him to please consider his family relationships and be respectful, but Hades is spiteful. It is a shame. So what do you need me to do?" She looked towards Mike and down at his sun necklace. "Son of Apollo? He was always one of my favorites, a very attractive boy and funny, too. He was always a little competitive for me, but he is a wonderful boy. He once killed a satyr because he played music as well as him. Oh goodness I have gotten off-track, my apologies."

"Lady Hestia," Brooke bowed, "we need your help to release the gods and to find Lady Artemis's huntresses." I laughed hearing her call me "Lady Artemis." The words just sounded weird coming out of her mouth. Hestia smiled and looked down on the three travelers.

"How can I say no to such adorable little heroes on such a noble quest? Follow me. Artemis's huntresses are in the shooting range on the west side of the mountain," she said as she pointed westward. She opened the back door and walked into the dazzling, golden sunlight. Large cherry trees hung over the pathway and the blossoms slowly floated to the ground around them. They walked down the side of the mountain and into a large field that held an ancient Greek arena. There was a large chariot track inside and a grassy field in the center with massive targets set up on one end. Nine archers stood in flowing, white dresses that danced around their ankles in the wind. Their arrows pierced perfect bulls-eyes from hundreds of meters away. Hestia clapped her hands twice, and they all dropped their weapons and bowed towards the goddess. I felt dread that I could not be there with my dear huntresses. They sweetly smiled and waved at Hestia. They critically eyed my friends. They averted their gaze from Mike and Landon while smiling at Brooke. "Hello, my dears. I have some friends I would like you to meet! This is... Oh my! I never got your names!"

"I'm Brooke, this is Mike and that is Landon! We are here to help Artemis," Brooke announced. My hunters looked them over carefully like they were prey we would stalk on a hunt. Then Channing, who is my best hunter, smiled.

"If you are trying to help Lady Artemis, we will be of service. Is she in some kind of trouble? What has happened?" Channing asked, looking uneasily at Mike and Landon as if they might be the cause.

"Hades has captured all the gods. He has locked them in indestructible cages, and he is raising the Titans. We need y'all to help us rescue them." The entire group of huntresses laughed and snickered when Mike said "y'all," but they composed themselves and nodded sternly at him. They looked to Hestia for direction. They had learned from me to only take orders from a woman, unless I told them otherwise.

"Well I assume Hades will have them locked up somehow, though I'm not aware of any material with the capacity to hold in a god." Hestia racked her brain for answers but came up short. "I do believe there are some other demigods that are trying to accomplish the same task as you are but without the sense to contact Olympus before charging the Underworld."

"We could meet with them, and then storm the Castel of Hades. It's a little risky, but there are a sufficient number of us." Amelia, one of my huntresses added.

"Agreed. To the Underworld! The huntresses grabbed Brooke's hands, and she quickly latched on to Mike and Landon. They formed a tight circle and waited for Hestia to make her way over. Hestia enclosed them in a warm glow, and with a burst of flames they were gone. Then my screen went black, and my heart ached.

# CHAPTER TWELVE

I stared back into the dark room of the Underworld, feeling hopeless. Suddenly, a loud pounding came from outside the large, back doors, and they burst into flames. I was amazed to see my huntresses with their bows drawn and their faces battle ready. Behind them stood my friends and several demigods I did not recognize. My mood soared as they walked in with their heads held high ready to take on the Underworld. One of my girls, Jane Everbrook, walked up to my cage and bowed. She looked sympathetically into my eyes and smiled. She grabbed the large lock and rubbed her hands across it. She dropped it immediately and stood back in shock. Her hand had momentarily turned wrinkled and grey. "My lady, I think only a mortal can open your cage. No hand of an immortal will break it. Thy cage is built of a substance which I can't understand." I nodded at her. Of course there was no way she could understand; no one had told her about Hades' evil creation and death was something she had never felt.

"The cage is sealed with death, which is why it ages you. I cannot leave the cage without dying, and since I am immortal, it's impossible for me to escape." My huntresses never argued with me, but I knew she did not agree with me. She looked at me quizzically and took several steps back. She took her bow and notched a silver arrow into the bow string. We watched her as she stared intensely at the lock and released her silver arrow into the keyhole of the diamond lock. When she released the arrow, the lock shattered and a deadly ear-piercing howl penetrated the room.

I pushed open the cage door timidly, not certain what would happen when I crossed the threshold. I took a step outside the cage, and my bare foot hit the icy ground. I shivered, but my foot did not age as it passed through the open door of the cage. The lock obviously housed the curse of death. The arrow had killed death itself. All the hunters gasped and collected their bows. One by one they shot the locks off each cage. With each shot another scream echoed through the walls. As we scrambled out of our cages, we were stopped by Hades' howling scream from outside the double, black doors. He stormed into the room, fuming as he saw the broken locks strewn across the marble floor.

"I see you believe you have discovered a way to escape? Perfect. I have succeeded at raising the Titans, so you are free to fight for your existence. I was coming to release you to your deaths anyway. They will come for you, all of you, and take your precious mountain. So go. Run, and enjoy what little time you have left with each other. But before you go I have someone who wants to see you."

From out of the shadows walked an enormous, muscular man. His face was tan and handsome but it was marred with horrible scars. One side of his mouth was forever contorted in a frown. I had not seen him in ages, but I recognized him as soon as he walked out as Prometheus.

"My dear friends, how long has it been since I was last in your company?" He laughed slightly, and then walked over to me and clasped my face in his enormous hands. He smiled at me, kissing me gently on the cheek. I could hear Landon growl from behind the huntresses. "Artemis, oh how you have grown! Do you remember when you used to sit on my lap, and I would tell you stories?"

"It has been so long, Prometheus. And of course, I remember," I said, smiling up at him. He had always been the father that Zeus had never been to me. Then Zeus sent him away. I had not seen him since the days when he was my friend, someone I could trust. I tried to appeal to him. "I have missed you. Are you sure you won't join our side? You are a father to me, and I will refuse to fight against you."

"My dear Artemis, you were always my daughter, but your real father must pay for what he did to me. I know what you have been offered, and I want you to think long and hard about it. Even if you lose this inevitable war, I will fight for your safety. Just think about it." He squeezed my hand, and then went around the room giving hugs and words of encouragement to all of those gathered. When he reached Zeus, his smile fell. "Zeus, I gave man what was necessary for him to advance, yet you punished me harshly. I molded man out of clay. I was their creator. This was all my design, not yours. Now you will pay for what you did to me. I will take you on myself, and you will surely perish". As he spoke, he lifted his massive arm and struck Zeus across the head. Zeus's large body was hurled to the floor. He hit the wall on the other side of the room, and the wall cracked. To everyone's shock, and Ares' dismay, no fight erupted. Zeus stood up and calmly walked back over to him and grabbed his shoulder.

"I am so sorry, Prometheus. I regretted it the second I left you there, but I could not take it back or my people would see me as weak. You were always a very close friend to me, and I know that I do not deserve your forgiveness. I am asking you for that forgiveness now, and I hope you will join us again." The whole room fell into an eerie silence. Had Zeus just apologized to Prometheus?

Prometheus turned back towards Zeus and nodded at him. Then he slowly walked off to the giant black doors and was gone.

I ran to the back of the room where my friends were standing. I hugged each one of them with all my strength. I thanked all my huntresses for their brave work. When I was done, I grabbed Brooke and apologized for causing her to have to stay down here. She would not hear it. In typical Brooke fashion, she thought it was a fun adventure and said she had never been in a cage before. Mike got a little emotional which made me smile. Tears slid down his face, and he babbled on about how he almost lost the two most important girls in his life. My conversation with Landon was awkward. He ran his hand through his hair and smiled at me. My heart still melted at his smile. Then he hugged me and pulled my face up to his.

"My little Bryn is actually a goddess. This will take some getting used to. I'm not surprised, though. There was always something different about you. I don't really know what else to say." He babbled on for awhile trying to find the right words, but with every utterance he stumbled even more. I stood on my tiptoes and kissed him, silencing all his confusion. I looked around and blushed. Thankfully everyone was too preoccupied to notice me. Everyone except Zeus. He walked toward me. He smiled at me as he turned both my shoulders towards the corner of the room. He steered me away from my friends who stood there looking confused. Apollo joined them and walked them to the other side of the room.

"Artemis, we have much to talk about. I will have Hestia guide your friends to their homes while we have a talk. Then you may go back and say your goodbyes. I have decided to cancel the mission in light of um... recent events. We need you back on Olympus." His voice wavered as he spoke. He was not accustomed to being trapped or having to apologize. It had been a rough day for him. For some reason I still found no room in my heart to pity him. I turned back to where my friends had stood, but they were gone. I was crushed, but I knew what I had to do. I followed Zeus back home.

We appeared inside Zeus's eight-story mansion. I stood in the foyer that was shining with diamonds and precious gems. I stepped barefoot on to the plush rugs and collapsed into one of the giant couches that sat on either side of the room. A small girl of about sixteen came in and brought me tea, which I finished in two gulps. I looked up to see Zeus looking at a portrait done by one of the muses of Apollo and me. "Now where did this little girl go?" He asked, turning to face me. His affectionate question seemed hollow; there was no real emotion in his voice.

"Zeus, spare me the sappy trip down memory lane. You never really cared for me back then anyway. Why am I really here?" I looked up at him with nothing but rage bubbling up inside my body. Zeus roared back with equal disdain, "This assignment was designed to test the vows of the gods. You probably don't remember, but when you took your vow to never be with a man, I gave you the option to back out whenever you wanted to. As time has passed, I thought it was time to reexamine the vows we took so many years ago. Our world has changed; it's different than it was when we took our vows. Humanity is supposed to be the ultimate emotional condition, so I decided to send you all down to examine yourselves and your vows from a different perspective. You have a decision to make, Artemis. Choose carefully. Once you break the vow, your choice is eternal." Zeus stopped talking and stared at me with a deep, penetrating look. I wasn't sure if his explanation of his experiment was true or not. It sounded too giving and without ego to be his motivation. I still didn't trust him. I glared back at him, trying to see if he would crack.

He continued his lecture, "The Titans are going to try to take their power back. I have not been the leader I need to be. That ends now. I will rule singularly from now on. You will all be demoted to minor gods after we win this war. All of the fighting we do amongst ourselves will stop when I reassert myself as the god of the gods, as it should be. You might choose to break your vow and become less of a goddess Artemis, but I plan to regain control and rule with all of the power bestowed upon me." At first I was shocked. All this time I had an option? I don't ever remember that as part of my vow. I was overcome with rage. How dare he try to take our power away because his own power was being threatened!

"Zeus, I don't know if you have noticed, but your plan did not exactly work out. Hades saw the weakness you created and decided to act on it. Now you are going to punish us all because you lost control by sending us on your errand? Apollo is in ruins from the death of his daughter, the Titans are rising, more mortals know about us, and we are on the brink of war. But you are wrong; we are stronger now. If we survive this war you can kiss your position of power goodbye. No one will listen to you when they find out what you did, and what you plan on doing. One apology will not save the world, and a million will not make up for the pain you have caused. If we fall, you will fall with us. We are still a team here. We must all make sacrifices. You must leave behind your vain, self-fulfilling ways, or we will all pay. Taking away our power will only make you weaker." My words came like venom. He looked at me as if seeing me for the first time.

"I would watch your words Artemis. You still have to come to me if you want your little friends down there to live. They will likely all be necessary sacrifices in this war anyway. We will have to save each other and my throne, so I am afraid your precious friends will not survive the war. You got too close, Artemis." He spat back, but pain was hidden behind his harsh words. "They know too much now anyway," he said with an evil look in his eye.

"So this is really it? This was part of your plan Zeus? It was all about you letting us loose and then regaining ultimate control? You are crazy if you think this plan will work. Kronos is a better option than you. You have to have followers in order to be a leader, Zeus. As soon as the others know what you are up to, no one will listen to you. You are worse than your brother Hades. You allowed Apollo's daughter to be killed in this, and you are willing to let the others die too? What have you become? You are a monster! You and Kronos are one and the same. You cut up your father and threw him out like a heap of trash. You both promised to not be like him, to rule differently, but you both ended up exactly what you didn't want to become."

With that, the lightning struck, aimed at me, but he missed and broke an ancient Greek vase that had been sitting on the shelves above my head. "I'm no longer your pawn. Power means nothing without people who believe in you, remember that. I will make Brooke my new huntress and you will work on your aim." I walked out of the room, turned around, pulled out my bow, and shot the cup he held in his hands. It shattered on the floor. "That's how you hit your mark," I huffed and then slammed the door behind me. Kronos might be right; Zeus had become just as bad as the Titans he had worked so hard to overthrow. It may be time for a new leader and a fresh start, but I don't think the new leader would or should be Kronos.

# Chapter Thirteen

I closed my eyes, and I stood in the pouring Texas rain outside Mike's house. The rain felt good in the hundred-degree weather. I felt a renewed strength and felt that nothing could bother me. I slowly trudged across the wet grass to the house. It stuck to the bottom of my bare feet and my hair was plastered to my forehead. Mike was sitting on the porch, but he did not notice me walk up. I set one wet hand on his shoulder and startled him.

"Oh Bryn, you're OK! I was so worried. Hestia said you were in grave danger." His forehead was creased with worry. I took my hand and smoothed the lines out of his face. I wavered on whether I should tell him what really happened. I stood there in front of him. I knew I had already put my life on the line and wasn't willing to do the same with his. His gleaming brown eyes had tears filling up the edges; I put my hand on his cheek and kissed his forehead.

"I think it's time Zeus got a taste of his own medicine. Call Brooke, Landon, and Apollo. It's time we stood up against him." I had an idea that would either get us all killed or would leave us as the most powerful beings in the universe.

"I don't need to call them, they are all inside. We have all been worried sick about you. What are you planning? Do you really think we can win against someone as powerful as Zeus?" His nervous questions required answers.

"He's not as powerful as he pretends to be. He operates from fear, that's the only reason people listen to him. Fear is his weapon, and he uses it powerfully. I have let go of my fear, and I can now stand on my own. It's time to make a deal with the devil, literally, and I know exactly how to reach him." My stomach churned. I had serious doubts that we could actually pull this off, but I couldn't let Mike see my hesitation. I told him I had let go of my fear, so I had to demonstrate confidence. I knew at a deep place inside myself that I had been waiting my whole life for this moment. I was not going to let it slip away now.

# Chapter Fourteen

"We are going to do what?" Apollo looked at like me like I had lost what little sanity I had left. Honestly, he was probably correct. We all knew Zeus must fall, that he had too much power. As we talked late into the night we compiled a list of reasons why we sought to overthrow him. We needed reasons if we were going to be able to convince the gods to join us. I wrote out a list for Apollo and the other gods to read. I handed the sheet of paper to Apollo. He eyed it slowly.

The Tyrant must go because:

- He kills more people than he saves.
- Anything he wants he takes, including people.
- He has taken credit for everyone else's achievements.
- We have little say in matters that affect our lives.

- The only person he thinks about is himself. He has never cared what happens to his brothers and sisters.
- He is the reason for human destruction.
- We have just as much power as he does. Why should we have to live under his strict laws?
- He has threatened to take away our power so that he may regain more control.
- He used us in his experiment to come live as humans to try to make us weaker.
- He is willing to sacrifice those most important to us to win his power.

The reasons to overthrow him would continue to grow as we rallied our forces. Our first blow would be at the next council meeting. We would stand in front of everyone and confront Zeus. It was the start of a revolution, and we would spearhead it. Our biggest problem, which I wasn't quite sure how to solve, was we still did not trust Hades. We weren't sure whose side he would land on, so we would need to play both sides of the fight. Each side would think we were on theirs, though in reality we would be on our own. We risked banishment, but sometimes that was worth what one believed in. The first person we called was Prometheus. He eagerly agreed in a matter of seconds. Now we had our first recruit. It was time to launch a war. Our immediate goal was to get Poseidon on our side. We needed at least one of the brothers if we had any hope to win. We hoped in the end that Poseidon and Prometheus would agree to rule side by side. People who did not desire power were the best to rule; they usually wouldn't take advantage of it.

I now stood on the edge of Mount Olympus. I went to see Zeus. He received me like an angry father receives a remorseful child. I apologized for overreacting and promised to attend the council meeting. He had little to say in response and dismissed me in a hurry. I wasn't sure if he knew I was playing him or not. I assumed he did, so I left his chamber as quickly as possible.

I then proceeded to tell Hades I was joining his team, but I asked that he not tell Zeus. He agreed and asked me if I would work with him to recruit Apollo. He believed the Titans were rising soon and wanted us both on his team. I assured him that Apollo would follow me wherever I went. In reality, Apollo and I were busy working with the other gods trying desperately to create the plan that would change everything.

I knew my huntresses would be critical for us to win any battle. Brooke had agreed to join the huntresses, and they were busy teaching her the skills of archery and battle. I gathered them together to address them. "My dear huntresses, I want to thank you for accepting our new huntress Brooke. She will be here with us while we fight. I know some of you have heard about my relationship with a mortal boy," they looked at each other uncomfortably at the mention of a boy. "It's true, and I have to take some time to reconsider my vow. His name is Landon, and he will help us in our fight against the Titans. What happens after that will be discussed after our battle. Are we all clear?" They nodded in unison.

Brooke got along well with the other huntresses. Her face glowed in the light of Olympus. A long silver dress flowed to her ankles, and she rubbed her thumb over the bow she had been given. I finally had ten hunters again. Zeus had seduced one my huntresses thousands of years ago, and I lost her. I had never thought of finding a new girl to take her place until now. Maybe I had shared too much with them, but they needed to trust me, and I had to let them know who Landon was before he joined our force. I dismissed them, and they all went back to work, preparing themselves for battle.

I slowly walked to the lake and sat on the dock. I pulled up my white dress and dipped my toes in the water. I started to trace large circles in the water with my toes until a pair of large hands grabbed my shoulders. I looked up to find Landon's face in mine. He smiled and sat down next to me. I blushed and smiled at him.

"When I did not know who you truly were, I made you blush and thought it was cute. Now it just confuses me. I have the power to make a Greek goddess blush. Promise me this whole uprising thing is not just because of me. I am going to have to fight, too, but we don't have to do it this way. You don't have to turn against your family." He looked down at the water.

"Landon, it's so much more than that. You don't know how long I have been waiting for this. You don't understand how horrible Zeus can be. If I don't do this you will die and the rest of us will lose our powers and be forced to be his slaves. The world as we know it will fall." I tried my best to describe something that sometimes even I didn't understand. Landon nodded and grabbed my hand. Although he nodded, I knew he would never truly understand. He had just learned about my world and was still trying to grasp it all; maybe throwing him into the beginnings of a war wasn't very smart. He took my chin in his hand, looked into my eyes and smiled. His smile certainly had power; maybe he could do this.

"Are you ready for all hell to break loose? This is war, Artemis. Many will die. Can you handle watching the ones you love die and betray you? You are going to have to be strong; war changes people. Can you be strong enough to stay yourself?" His words echoed in my head. For a mortal, he sure understood a lot. I kissed him and then stood up. I needed to see my brother.

I walked away slowly past the beautiful fields and growing Ambrosia. The golden plants sparkled in the sunlight. I walked a bit further into an open-air courtyard. Small silver rocking chairs sat on a small slab of marble. Beautiful flowers encircled the sitting area. I saw Apollo outside the courtyard sitting on a checkered blanket with a fire burning beside him. He had a guitar strapped across his bare chest, and he played ancient music. His head was bent over his guitar, and his eyes were closed as he played numbly. The tune changed multiple times. I could tell he wasn't really paying attention to the music but was lost in his own thoughts. I walked up to him and put my hand on his strong back that was warm from the sun. He looked up at me with his pained eyes. He had never been good with conflict; it was always better for him if everyone and everything was happy.

"Artemis, I have been thinking about this whole battle. Are you sure we will be able to pull this off? What if nobody wants to join? What will we do?" The pain and fear enveloped him.

"We hope they will want to join us. We know many are just as tired of Zeus as we are; they know what he plans on doing to all of us when this war is over. If no one joins us that doesn't mean we quit. We stick to it, and it will only be a matter of time before they see what we see. Until then, we give 'em hell." He nodded and absently strummed a few chords on his guitar. He gave me a hug, humming a song that our mom used to sing to us when we were little. He knew I was in as much pain as he was, and I was glad I had him here to help me. For that moment I remembered feeling human. I missed being Bryn and the fun I had on earth with Brooke and my friends. I didn't want to be Bryn, but I enjoyed being her for the brief time I was there. Bryn helped me find Artemis.

I stood up after a few minutes and slowly walked back to my house. It was a giant gleaming white, marble structure that was four stories high. Each room represented a different country I had been to and loved. The rooms boasted different animals I had seen. They were not stuffed, they were fully alive, and I had made them immortal and obedient so I could keep them as pets. A Bengal tiger that I had found in India prowled through the living room, a white tailed deer I had acquired from Canada was curled up by the door, and there was a giant panda rummaging through the kitchen. I stood in the kitchen and grabbed a giant pad of paper and a gold pen. I went up to my bed to write my speech for the council meeting. We were not sure when the meeting would be called, but it could be as soon as tomorrow. After a few minutes with my pen in my hand, I drifted off into another fitful sleep where Kronos found his way to invade my mind.

In my dream, I stood in a large empty field, which looked like the fields of Asphodel but without all the twittering ghosts. Kronos stood beside me. He was dressed in full armor looking like he had gained all his strength. The sight of him gave me the chills. The legends of his battle crimes were horrific. I had been young then, and they had kept Apollo and me away from the more powerful Titans.

He walked toward me and ran his fingers through my long, dark hair. Stroking my face, he smiled. "My dear, I am so glad we finally get to meet. It is always a shame when a grandfather can't see his grandchildren." He smiled wickedly at me. "I hear you have joined us, though I can sense that your true allegiance lies elsewhere. I also know you hate Zeus almost as much as I do. For whom are you truly willing to fight?" He searched me over as though the answer he was looking for was hidden in the folds of my dress.

"Myself. I want my dreams to be realized. I don't completely agree with what either side wants. I want to see Zeus fall more than I want to see you locked up." I lied, and I could sense that he knew I was not telling the truth. He said nothing. He just nodded.

"You are so different from the others. I do not hate you. You see through lies, and I like that. I respect you for it. But chasing only your wants and desires can be a dark road. Do not make me kill you my dear. It would be a definite loss." He laughed darkly, and then I fell into a dreamless sleep.

When I awoke the next morning I was in a dark mood. I had decided to spend the day in my garden hoping it would improve my mood. Flowers filled every inch of the grounds and cherry blossom trees lined my yard. It was a perfect hunting ground with almost every type of terrain. I hunted in the morning and then spent the rest of the day lying on a blanket by the small river that snaked through my yard, aiming my arrows at any poor animal that happened to stroll too close.

"Bryn?" Brookes' voice startled me. The fact she was here at my home still made me smile. It was nice to have a true friend. "I was talking to Apollo, and he said you might be out here. It's very beautiful. He also told me a story about when y'all were little how you used to make pictures out of the clouds. Would you show me?" She laughed and sat down next to me. Her bright red hair fell into her face. I nodded and turned towards the sky holding up my hands. With simple movements of my hands, creatures formed from the clouds. First, I created a dog, then a bear, then a stag. I watched Brooke's pleased reaction and advanced to more exotic creatures like a Satyr, a Cyclops, and a python. I wiped the sky slate clean and watched the amazement on Brooke's face. As the animals disappeared, she slowly came back to reality.

"Did you like that? I have a lot of tricks I could show you now that you are here. I just wish we had more time," I whispered. "I loved that! That was amazing, but near the end they started to look more like frogs." I pretended to look hurt, but really I was just glad she was here. Then she sat up, grass sticking up in the back of her hair. Her face grew somber, and she said, "It will all work out you know. I promise it will all be OK in the end." She gave my hand a tight squeeze.

After a few minutes of sitting together in silence I could smell Apollo approaching behind me. His distinct strong, sweet scent drifted through the trees. His eyes were stormy and his mouth was set in a deep frown. Mike was walking behind him, with his head held low. "It's time, Artemis. The council meeting is going to start in ten minutes." His tone held no emotion, as if he was numb to the world. As he spoke, my good mood evaporated as quickly as the clouds. The four of us started back along the dirt road leading through the forest toward the city.

As we walked through the stone streets of Olympus, I could see the fountains bubbling happily. Little cherubs were flying through the air singing softly and playing their harps. The grass gleamed perfectly in the sunlight. Brooke shined as a new huntress, and her bow was strapped to the back of her beautiful hunting dress.

I walked with purpose, practicing the words I would say at the council meeting. I harnessed some of my human emotion, which helped fuel me. I used my anger to fuel my body. I had enough inside of me to fuel the Spartan Army.

Soon the beautiful brass doors of the hall of the gods came into view. I knew it was time; I would have to harness everything strong and purposeful inside me to be successful. I had to be the best of Artemis and the best of Bryn to save us all.

# CHAPTER FIFTEEN

We stood in the Great Hall of the gods, and I slowly made my way over to my usual seat and stared blankly at Apollo from across the room. "My dear family," bellowed Zeus as he walked into the room with Hera linked to his arm. "I'm so glad to have you all back. We have a lot to do if we want to defeat the Titans." His eyes twinkled as he spoke in a sinister tone. Everyone nodded, but no one shared his enthusiasm. The gods looked defeated and scared. Zeus gloated. I would do everything in my power to send Zeus and his new plan crumbling down.

Zeus started to speak of our defensive strategies. At random points Athena or Ares would argue, but the room was otherwise very silent. Zeus started to feel tension building. He stopped talking about war abruptly. "What's going on?" His eyes were filled with rage. Apollo and I stood up in unison, and everyone took in a sharp breath. This was unheard of. As soon as we stood, the doors to the hall burst open and in walked all ten of my huntresses. Following the pack of stunning huntresses were Mike and Landon looking overwhelmed and a confident Prometheus following behind. Brooke led the huntresses with her red hair piled on top of her head and her bow slung over her shoulder.

"Well my dear," I spat back sarcastically. It was time for me to shine. "This is what you would call an uprising. My fellow gods and goddess, we all know we have been oppressed by Zeus for a very long time. His power is beginning to wane, so he is desperate, grasping to regain all of his command over us. His plan is to dominate us completely." Many nodded their heads in agreement. "If we win, he plans to take away most of our powers and demote us to minor gods so that he may rule more forcefully. That's why he sent us to live with mortals; he wanted us to become weaker, like humans. He wasn't hoping to make us stronger by connecting us to human emotion. He was hoping to weaken us. This tyrant will stop at nothing to take over completely. If we don't stop him now, will he become as bad as the ruler he fought so hard to overthrow in the first place? Or is he already there?" Shocked gasps echoed through the hall. Zeus was so stunned, he couldn't move.

"We have compiled a list of reasons why we think we should overthrow him. Each of you is free to decide. You can stay with Zeus and be no more than his minion or you can join the Titans and watch the world you worked so hard to create be destroyed. Or you can join us." I motioned behind me, "You can overthrow two evil groups, and we can do remarkable things. I'm not looking for power. In fact, I was hoping Poseidon would take that position. All of you know me well enough to know that I am about the hunt, not about the glory. But when he starts to threaten the lives of the ones I love, I will not sit here and watch. We need you to join us, if we have any chance. It is time. I invite those of you willing to do what is right to stand with me." For a moment no one moved in the hushed hall. Everyone looked as shaken and speechless as Zeus. Slowly the blank stares were replaced with excitement and energy. The first to stand up was Athena. She turned back to Zeus and told him, "For many years I have used my wisdom and knowledge to make the right decisions for this empire, and now I see the correct path is not the one you travel. I must leave if I wish to retain my own sanity." Then she walked over, squeezed my hand and stood behind Apollo.

The next to stand was Poseidon. He whipped his head around and faced Zeus. "I will no longer follow my little brother and be treated like a second-class citizen. You don't deserve the power you have. You haven't earned it; you have simply taken it." Poseidon stormed down the marble steps toward us and stood his ground. With Poseidon, we were now 17 strong. We stood waiting for the next god to join our cause. Hermes stood up next saying he would always follow Apollo. He gave Apollo a thankful smile. Hephaestus stood next and declared his allegiance to us because his mom had thrown him off Olympus as a baby. We accepted him lovingly and were happy to have another god join us. Hestia looked hurt by her family breaking apart and announced she would be taking no sides and slowly exited the room crying.

Suddenly Zeus snapped out of his confusion and a giant lightning bolt erupted. It struck me in the chest. I flew back and hit the back wall knocking over one of his many statues. "I worked on my aim, dear, how does it feel? Artemis you have made the biggest mistake of your life. You will all pay for what you are doing, but for now get off of Olympus!" He screamed the last words. Apollo picked me up and steadied me with his strong arms.

A large boom fired through the halls and the world turned black and silent. The next thing I knew, we were all standing on the lawn in front of Mike's house. All 19 of us gods, demigods, and mortals were awkwardly standing in the blazing sun of the human world. We had been kicked off Olympus and the biggest fight of our lives stood before us.

I knew I had started something, something greater than I could imagine. There was no turning back now. I had thrown everyone I cared for into a monumental war that would change each of us forever. I was afraid some of us would die, but I couldn't focus on that now. Fear weakened me, and I knew I needed every ounce of strength within me to win this war.

"What do we do now?" mumbled Hephaestus. "We plan. We stay strong and plan our first attack," stated Athena confidently. I looked at them; I knew I had to make the decision. I needed to lead them. I also knew we were not ready to attack yet. We definitely needed time to plan. I knew what we had to do.

It was my turn to lead. I was ready, so I confidently commanded, "No, now we rally our troops. It's time to gather an army even the Titans will fear. The war begins now."